Forever Beth
Our Love

By:
Elizabeth Cook-Howard

Book Two
of the
Forever Beth Series

Elizabeth Cook – Howard
Forever Beth Our Love

Elizabeth Cook – Howard is a fulltime professional in the social services field, wife and mother to four beautiful children. Born and raised in Queens New York she moved to the Lower Hudson Valley Region of New York to raise her family. Creating and writing mystery and love stories since her teens it wasn't until her early forties she decided to pen and self-publish her work, hence the ***Forever Beth Series*** first ***Lost and Found*** and now ***Our Love.***

Acknowledgement and Dedication

My wonderful children Quentin, Angelica, Joshua and Ashley It warms my heart to know you're my biggest fans... Know and Trust I am yours always.

My husband, my usual thank you. I like you on most days but love you on all days.

My parents Frank and Patricia. Daddy I know you're watching every day from heaven. Not a day goes by that I don't think of you. My mother who in so many ways I am like growth, patience and understanding. I love you.

And last but not least my sisters and brother as we get older, always "One Love"

Table of Contents

Wherefore they are no more twain, but one flesh. What therefore God hath joined together, let not man put asunder.

Matthew 19:6

Prologue:

My baby girl, love as you know doesn't come all that easy. When you find it you must cultivate it, water it and even fertilize it every day and the love you share with another will flourish. But love is never without challenges just as life isn't without consequences. When you gain the will, conquering will be a battle easily won. Love, respect and honor yourself first and always be genuine. By doing so allows others to love and respect you for who you are and in return the truth of love for which you seek will be found. Listen to your heart and learn from mistakes made. Now open your eyes and see the love that has been waiting a lifetime for you. I love you baby girl... Always with you. Always!

Chapter One: New Beginnings

I can stare at this same scene for the rest of my life. My husband of not even a full twenty four hours only dressed in a pair of basketball shorts and a tank. His caramel glistening skin being enhanced by the stream of sunlight flooding in through the open terrace doors. He sits with legs crossed, a cup of coffee in one hand and another novel in the other. My waking eyes prompt the ever so smile on my face. Trying to move as little as possible, I twist a bit to allow for an even better view. But my seemingly minimal adjustment catches the attention of "my man" and with an ever so large smile he makes his way to me.

Good morning Mrs. Walker, my wife how did you sleep?

The best rest I ever experienced *I can't contain the extra-large smile emerging on my face.*

You do the same for me beautiful!

Oh this man… What are you doing up so early?

Not so early, going on 2:00 p.m.

Can't be

Oh it is

Why didn't you wake me?

Wake you, why? We are on our honeymoon. No agenda, no schedule to keep to. Besides with us flying in so late you needed the rest.

What about you?

Baby, I'm well rested and enough about me *Kevin walks back out to the living-room area, he returns with a tray* tea and croissants?

Oh yes, this looks absolutely delicious *taking one of the croissants* and my favorite, chocolate thank you! So what is on our non-existent agenda for today?

I thought we would enjoy this private suite for today and begin exploring the island if you like tomorrow.

Oh Mr. Walker I like the way you think. So does that mean you will be climbing back into bed?

Oh it does....

Kevin walks to the edge of the bed, pulls his tank up and over his head. Oh god how beautiful this man is. He proceeds to pull off his NBA shorts, the last piece of clothing covering this statue of a man. Seeing him completely nude, I cannot contain myself any longer. Meeting him at the edge of the bed I whisper "I'm so lucky to have you" *and I begin kissing this man, initially slowly on his lips. Taking my time kissing his beautiful chest, I take in his scent. Moving further down Kevin's body just at the right speed to enhance his curiosity, I Stop at the lower end of his stomach. Looking up to see Kevin's reaction, eyes are closed. I Move further down his body ending at his manhood. Looking up at him once more, Kevin is staring down at me with a look of "are you really about to do this"? My eyes answers and I take Kevin into my mouth.*

Whispering "Beth"

Kevin saying my name excites me even more, sparking a need to do this to the best of my ability, trying with great difficulty to have all of him in my mouth. But the more I force him in the larger he grows. Overwhelmed, Kevin in one flash pulls himself out of my mouth picks me up, positions me onto the bed and instantly inside me. I'm experiencing an excitement that I can't ever recall feeling. The more this man thrust the more I want him. Uncontrollably tears begin trickling down my face and I grab Kevin even tighter. I now find myself meeting his thrust with a thrust. My body has total control. Then it happens, something I've never experienced before, I cum? Not metaphorically, I felt it I feel it and if I stand I know I will see it. What the hell! And in response to my body's appeasement Kevin strains the words "oh Beth I love you" *and just then I feel for the first time ever, a man exploding inside me. The intensity sparks further excitement within me, responding with an overwhelming – intense disbursement. Oh My God..... What just happened? Looking at me, Kevin becomes alarmed by the tears that just won't stop.*

Beth what's wrong? Did I do something? Did I hurt you?

Tears falling faster, none of the above Kevin, I've never known this level of happiness before and this *waving my hands over our naked bodies* never once have I experienced such pleasure.

So you now understand how I feel *said with such sincerity.*

I'm sure you had your share of women

Interrupting me, whatever I may or may not have had, I never had you. Baby I wish you knew what you do to me and for me. I've never wanted anyone so much in my life until the first day I laid eyes on you. *Kevin's voice pressing with that familiar tone of concern.* If anything was to ever happen to you my life would be over.

Climbing onto Kevin's lap and putting my arms around his neck the only way you wouldn't have me would be you kicking me to the curb. *I begin laughing* Sorry to say you're stuck with me!

Then stuck for life I am *Kevin begins kissing me*

Oh no you don't, Mr. Walker

No, what? Why? *Smiling*

No meaning no hanky panky!

Laughing why?

Why - really? Did you see what you just did to me?

Correction, do you know what you just did to me? *Both of us laughing*

Well Mr. Walker until I recover, how about a nice walk with your wife on the beach and if you're lucky and if we stumble upon a nice quiet secluded spot, a repeat from a few minutes ago?

Mrs. Walker, really? *Sporting a large smile* I'm all for it!

Then let's get this party started. *I begin to laugh, climbing off of Kevin's lap. Just then the phone rings and Kevin answers. I mouth* "going to take a shower" *Kevin smiles and I leave the room.*

Must be the tropical air, standing under, in and over this amazing shower water coming from every direction I feel a sense of pure calmness. I close my eyes and allow each drop of water to hit me, falling so comfortably onto my body. The peacefulness emitting from within me I begin to revisit what just happened, I shiver. I feel Kevin's soft sensual hands caressing my back, moving to the front of me and ending at my breast. I feel him massaging each very slowly but forcefully. I feel my legs parting, making way for him. I feel him inside me and I hear him whispering my name in my ear. I must be losing it because this feels too real. Calling my name once again my body reacts. In this moment I realize I'm not alone.

Baby I love you

Responding instantly I love you too Kevin *and with these words my body releases. Kevin reacting to my blatant satisfaction, he too releases grabbing me tighter and holding on.*

Barely able to stand on my own, Kevin swoops me off my feet and carries me from the shower to the bed. With a smile on his face, I'm kissed.

I can't take too much more of this. Now you're affecting my ability to stand on my own?

Oh but Beth, so much more is ahead of us.

Like what?

All in due time Mrs. Walker. All in due time! *And with a large smile Kevin begins to dress*

Kevin who called?

The front desk

Why?

Oh nothing really, Erickson faxed some info to me.

Info on what?

Beth nothing important, just something he and I were working on.

Okay?

I need to go down and review what he sent. I'll only be a few minutes.

Well you go on, just remember what will be waiting for you

Oh baby….

About to put on my one piece bathing suit. Maybe I should wear my two piece?

One piece or two, it's all coming off. *The words alone makes me squirm.*

Walking along the shore line I'm appreciating a few minutes of me time. Taking in the beautiful sights around me, I take a seat and allow the gentle waves to splash into me. If anyone would have told me how warm the water was on the 2nd of January I would plainly say "lie". But experiencing first hand I now know paradise actually exists. Oh how beautiful it is. Sitting here I'm reminded of my interactions with God, my father, Rosie and Rosa. Looking to the heavens that calm I think I experienced some months back is being mimicked right this second. I close my eyes and think back to a few days ago, my beautiful wedding. I smile at the thought of Kevin holding me in his arms. Then a flash, daddy comes into focus and by surprise Rosie and Rosa are standing with him. Each of them smiling and waving hello. With my eyes still closed I raise my hand and wave back. Walking slowly away from me while still waving, I hear Kevin whispering in my ear "Are you okay?" *I'm brought back to the here and now, back to reality.*

Everything is just fine. Are you all done?

All done baby *taking a seat next to me* why are you sitting here?

Look, *gesturing to look straight in front of us* look how beautiful this is. This could be heaven.

So Mrs. Walker I did well in choosing a honeymoon site?

Oh yes you did. But …

But what Beth?

The cost of the trip. Kevin ……

Beth what's bothering you?

I can't allow you to keep spending on me. We need to discuss finances

Beth?

Kevin, not once have you asked anything of me. When we go out it becomes a battle for me to pay for anything. You flood me with gifts that I could never afford to buy and let's not forget our magnificent wedding, this gorgeous suite, flying here first class, assuming going back the same way and this *looking down at my wedding rings*. We need to talk about our finances.

Beth??

And let's not forget my little man, Tiger… Stray cat that needed a home? Really? The vet confirmed him being a pure breed Savannah, questioning how I was able to purchase such a breed when the starting cost is $4000!

Beth I told you no lies. I stated he needed a home and he did.

Kevin really?

Beth your money is your money.

((Absolutely Not)) our marriage needs to be a partnership, nothing less!

So what do you propose?

Share expenses!

Okay. Now can we change the subject?

No Kevin you are not just going to dismiss this topic. And your "okay" is as believable as Elvis being alive.

Beth, look at that beautiful view. Do you really want to have this debate right now?

Yes I do. First know with the promotion my salary will be about seventy thousand a year. I came into this marriage with debt, my debt. I have student loans, car note and rent!

Smiling Beth I didn't marry you for your money.

Not funny Kevin

Trying to hold back a smile Beth, I do okay for myself, I plan well. If you decided to stop working right this second we would be okay.

You know that would never happen.

I'm just saying! Beth financially we are okay. But since we are on the subject *pulling his wallet out and taking out two credit cards* for you.

A Barclay's Visa and American Express? Kevin are you kidding me?

Beth take the cards, please. No big deal, I just added you to my accounts.

Kevin..... Do you see what I mean?

Beth what? *Sounding annoyed*

Kevin I don't want you to take care of me. I walked that road before *my voice begins to crack.* I don't need nor want anyone taking care of me.

Grabbing me firmly by the shoulders Beth do not ever compare me to your past. Do not interpret what I do for you, my wife as having motive. What I am able to do will be done.

Turned on, pissed and overwhelmed. Everything I'm feeling this very moment Kevin I don't want you taking care of me.

Loosing up on his grasp Beth if you were at home right now suffering from the flu would you be opposed to me taking care of you? Your every need?

Come on Kevin, not the same.

It is. But the cards are in your name, you do as you see fit.

Taking the cards in hand, I look at the name. He nailed it! Elizabeth Cook-Walker, how did you know I would hyphenate?

Baby you don't give me enough credit.

Sighing No I don't..... *Leaning over and kissing Kevin* something I will work on immediately but you too need to take what I'm saying seriously. I don't want to be financially taken care of. Partners correct?

Yes we are.

Then treat me as such. No more expensive gifts! Right now I think you and I should be saving for a house?

Finally we can agree on something. I was hoping we could begin to look when we get back?

Sure but *laughing* where do we stay when we get back?

I was thinking we could stay at my / our place. Why?

Baby you have a beautiful apartment

But???

But my apartment is a bit larger, three bathrooms and I own not rent.

Hmmm

Hmmm?

Just hmmm! Please do not take this personally but Kevin your apartment isn't homely, not lived in.

True but I thought I've been changing that?

Yes you have. I especially love the pictures of you and I on the wall.

Baby even when you think I'm not listening, I am.

And that is why I married you.

It wasn't for my handsome looks *profiling*

That too... *Laughing*

So is it settled, you will be moving into our apartment?

Yes but Kevin I need to see if I can break my lease.

Don't worry about the lease.

Don't start Mr. Walker......

Ok ok.... *throwing his hands into the air. Standing Kevin holds out his hand to help me up.* Now can I have my first dinner with you as my wife?

You sure can once I had my dessert.

Mrs. Walker......

Chapter Two – Inseparable

Mrs. Walker how are you enjoying your honeymoon so far?

I'm loving every second of it. But Mr. Walker as long as I am with you anywhere would be heaven.

Baby I feel the same way.

Putting myself across Kevin's lap and laying my head on his bare chest as he lays back on the couch. So what should we do this fine evening?

Looking down at his watch I'm glad you asked that question. *Just then a knock at the door.*

Beth that would be for you!

Huh?

Baby get the door please?

Kevin what are you up to?

Putting his shirt and sandals on Not a thing…

Answering the door I am face to face with a beautiful island woman Hello!

Good afternoon, Mrs. Walker?

I am

Mrs. Walker we *(referring to about three other women standing behind her)* are here to help you get ready for this evening.

Excuse me?

Kevin now standing on the side of me Beth Pascale is here to help you get prepared for this evening.

Kevin? *Whispering* help with what?

A formal evening with your husband.

Kevin what? Formal? How formal?

Beth don't worry everything you need is here. Be ready by seven. Pascale knows the plan and she is sworn to secrecy *flashing that handsome smile.*

I'm going to kill you.

Luckily I have nine lives…..

Kevin can I talk to you in the bedroom?

Nope….. Pascale my beautiful wife is all yours. Remember, be ready promptly at seven!

Kissing me, Kevin quickly leaves and I am left alone and in the hands of four strange women.

Mrs. Walker I manage the spa here at the resort. Mr. Walker requested my services which includes a massage, facial, hair, nails and the assistance of dressing for this evening.

How much is all this?

Mrs. Walker, Mr. Walker instructed me not to review any cost.

Listen I appreciate this but sorry I'm not interested.

Mrs. Walker, Mr. Walker said you would attempt to refuse services and if you did I am to call him immediately.

Are you kidding me?

No, but I assure you he has a very special evening planned.

Shaking my head whatever, let's just do this and get it over with. *With what seems like a forced smile Pascale and her crew begins.*

After about three hours I've been massaged, pedicured, manicured, face scrubbed, rubbed and peeled, scented from my exotic milk bath, hair done and now to be dressed. I head into my bedroom but stopped by Pascale.

Mrs. Walker where are you going?

Pascale? I'm going to see if I have anything close to formal with me. Do you have any idea how formal I need to be?

Well by Mr. Walker's instructions - very formal which is why he requested that I bring a few items from the resort's boutique.

You are kidding me right?

No *and just then three garment bags appear and dresses taken out of each.*

Wait, the gowns are absolutely stunning but *checking each for a price tag* I'm sure they are out of my price range!

Mrs. Walker each have already been purchased, you just need to choose one for this evening.

About to go off, the phone rings Hello?

Beth you have exactly thirty minutes to be ready.

Kevin did we not just have a discussion yesterday about finances? Remember on the beach? You and me?

Beth I will not have this discussion with you right now. Please just get ready. A car will be picking you up exactly at seven. *The line goes dead. No goodbye, no I love you. Nothing... This son of a bitch.*

Mrs. Walker everything okay?

Yes....

Which gown?

I don't care – it doesn't matter.

Could I make a suggestion?

I guess

You would look absolutely stunning in this one *pointing to a champagne colored – mermaid style gown.*

Sure *confirming my choice sparks a mass production, each of the women grabbing, tucking and placing something on me. By the time all is done I'm escorted to the full length mirror in the bathroom. Seeing myself I immediately dismiss my dislike of how this evening came about. I look at Pascale with tears in my eyes* You really know how to clean someone up.

Mrs. Walker no clean-up, I just enhanced the beauty that is already present.

Well thank you very much!

You are welcome. But you must get going. Your carriage awaits out front.

Packing the purse that matches this stunning dress I head to the door. Pascale thank you!

Mrs. Walker we will pack up and insure your suite is back in order. Enjoy your evening.

Stepping out of the suite I'm greeted by an older gentleman with a heavy Caribbean accent Good Evening Mrs. Walker my name is Peter and I will be your driver this evening.

Good Evening Peter. *Walking with Peter I am led to a beautiful Cinderella type carriage that is driven by six stunning white horses. Literally a carriage.* For me?

Yes for you!

Once seated in the carriage Peter hands me a sealed envelope. Mrs. Walker, Mr. Walker requested you open and review the contents before we depart.

Opening the envelope I pull out a note on the most exquisite parchment paper which reads:
This evening is my wedding gift to you, my wife. I love you baby with all I have. Enjoy this evening without any worries or doubts. I await your arrival.
 Love, Kevin......

Hold back the tears Beth, ya going to mess up three hours of hard work. He has to stop doing this!

Mrs. Walker shall we go.

With tears falling, Yes Peter thank you.

As Peter proceeds to where I have no idea, I think of Kevin and how much this man makes me so very happy. Who knew this level of happiness could be. In this moment I find myself humming Natalie Cole's "I've Got Love On My Mind". I close my eyes and hear her words internally. But why does the music in

*my head seem to get louder and louder? I open my
eyes as the carriage comes to a complete stop. In
front of me my husband dressed in a black tuxedo -
looking ever so handsome. He greets me by extending
a hand to help me down. I look my husband in his
eyes and whisper* "I love you so much".

Baby, I know the feeling!

*In this moment I realize the noise in my head is
actual. Kevin takes my hand and guides me to a
gazebo on the beach. A live band is playing I've Got
Love on My Mind and the kicker, my husband begins
to sing as we dance. Oh my God, is this real? And he
can sing! What the hell, I'm melting away.*

I've got love on my mind… I've got love on my
mind

And there's nothing' particularly wrong, It's a feeling'
I feel inside

When I woke up early this morning, It was staring'
me straight in my eyes

When you touch me I can't resist

And you've touched me a thousand times

When I think of your tender kiss

He's singing this to me??? Oh my God!!

Then and there I start to unwind

In your arms I like to be, Caressing' you gentle and
tenderly

From sunrise to sunset, All through the day

I've been waiting for your return

And you know this is where I'll be

I can say to the world I've learned

Only you can satisfy me…. Satisfy me

Oh you have made me, so very happy

Mrs. Elizabeth Lillian Walker

The flood begins, I can't stop crying. Kevin taking me completely into his arms, I'm reminded of his strong sensual touch. My heart skipping a beat as it has so many times before from his touch. I hear a woman now singing "Inseparable". What is this man trying to do to me?

Continuing to dance, Kevin kisses my neck, my cheek and then my forehead. I lay my head against his chest and take in his scent which reminds me of the evening I decided to give myself to him. I close my eyes and listen to the words, words that express how I feel about my man. Kevin caressing my lower back whispers in my ear

"You and I are inseparable. I can't imagine not having you in my life".

The only response I could possibly give, I look up at Kevin and kiss him with all the passion in me. Pulling away "Mr. Walker, I never knew what true happiness was until you". *Just then the song ends and the band begins playing another tune. Kevin takes my hand and escorts me to a secluded seating area.* Mr. Walker you did all this?

All for you!

Thank you.

No, thank you for allowing my eyes to see such beauty. Baby you look absolutely stunning.

I was about to say the same about you *because dam you look GOOD!* But Kevin your note, wedding gift – all this, baby you have given me so much.

Well this is my gift. And please don't bring up finances.

Kevin for once, right this moment finances isn't even a thought.

Really? Then what is?

You!

I like that….. What about me?

Just how happy you make me. How you fulfill me in every way.

Oh Mrs. Walker!

Really….. Listen to me Kevin, you complete me in every way. I never knew this type of happiness existed. Mentally and physically, you complete me!

No you have it twisted baby, you complete me….. Now *standing and extending his hand for mine* let's see what the chef prepared for us.

Leading the way Kevin and I walk to the pier where a boat is docked.

Kevin are you kidding me?

No baby I'm not. Onboard dinner awaits.

Following Kevin, I am steered to an upper deck where a beautiful table is set for two. Sitting, Kevin and I barely touch our food. We talk for over an hour while looking into each other's eyes. The conversation, our love and our life expectations. Looking at his watch Kevin motions me to get up, he takes my hand and we walk to the back of the boat.

Watching the sun just hovering and the moon peeping through is priceless.

It sure is. *Shaking my head as in disbelief* Paradise absolutely exist.

Beth are you familiar with Japanese paper lanterns?

No I can't say I am.

The Japanese have an annual summer festival called Feast of Lanterns or Festival of the dead. Over a three day period the Japanese conducts a cleansing of their ancestors graves and homes. Basically honoring them. The lanterns are lit and placed in the local waterways to guide the spirits home. Now it isn't something I completely believe in but I certainly like the meaning behind it. I thought this evening, although not summer and obviously not in Japan, I thought together we could light lanterns and watch each move with the waves. If anything letting the people we cared about know we are thinking of them.

Kevin I would love to.

Exiting the boat, Kevin and I walk back to the Gazebo where four lanterns sit.

For your father, my mom, Rosie and Rosa.

Together lighting each, the four beautiful Japanese lanterns are placed into the water. In silence we stand for many minutes watching each head for the open ocean. Wrapped in my husband's arms that familiar feeling of content sets in.

Kevin tonight, thank you. I loved every second.

I'm glad because it isn't over.

Kevin it is late. All I want to do is make love to my man and lay in his arms...

Really?

Really!

Taking my hand into his follow me.

Following Kevin, we go back onto the boat but this time below deck and enter a beautiful cabin with pink and red rose petals everywhere and champagne on a tray that sits perfectly on the bed with strawberries.

We will be lodging here tonight.

Kevin?

No argument!

But I didn't bring anything!

You didn't need to. I took care of it.

Knock..... Knock...... *Kevin opens the door*

Mr. Walker should we set out?

Yes... *Kevin closing the door*

Kevin we are going to sail or whatever you call it?

Yes we are. Not too far out don't worry.

Kevin not worried or concerned. *I turn for Kevin to unzip my gown. Stepping out of it Kevin un-hooks my bra and begins kissing my back. I turn to face him and I remove his jacket, then his shirt. Continuing, I undo his pants and pull them down and without missing a beat Kevin steps out of them. I remove my panties and meet Kevin in the middle of the floor. Suddenly I find myself dancing with my husband but to what? The band? I ask no questions, for once in my life I'm going with the flow and right now that flow has me dancing completely nude on a boat with a band playing in the background with a man who loves me as I him. Heavenly father if I haven't thanked you I am this very moment, thank you for bringing this man to me. Thank you for putting him into my life. Daddy don't look down at me right this moment... please don't. But know your baby girl finally found happiness, but I think you already know that! I look up at Kevin, into his eyes and smile with tears of joy falling* Inseparable we are. I Love You!

Chapter Three – Now You Know

Our last day in paradise, Kevin and I head back tomorrow. Disappointed a little but I can't wait to get back and see my loving sister Cynthia and save her from my psychotic cat as she puts it. But more importantly I'm excited to return to work on Monday as "Director". I love the title but it just hit me, I should look like a director. I guess I can do some shopping Sunday while Kevin is at work. But for right now I need to pick up a few souvenirs. I can only imagine the prices in this gift shop but for the people I am purchasing for is well worth it.

Good afternoon

Hello

Can I help you find something?

No, just looking.

Please let me know if you need any assistance.

Thank you I will.

My lord, just what I imagined look at the prices! Okay let's start with Rochelle. Yes this paperweight with an interactive beach scene imbedded would be great. Working at the Mayor's office she will need some type of daily serenity reminder. The Mayor's office, huh. It just hit me, Rochelle will not be with me on Monday when I return to work. I will never be able to fill her shoes, I just hope I meet the board's expectations. Ah this would be perfect for Cynthia, a beautiful sea glass pendant necklace. For Paige, hmmm what do you get the youngest woman in the agency or better yet barely twenty one year old with legs a mile long, the looks of a model and a body to go with it? Yes this sarong would look great on her. Catching my eye now, a leather bracelet with three shells that read "I love you" perfect for Kevin. And this very large seashell for Adele and John. Well, all done. Time to see the damage! I make my way to the counter.

Mrs. Durand did you find everything you were looking for?

Turning to see who this woman is talking to. No one behind or on the sides of me. Sorry are you talking to me?

Yes Mrs. Durand

Sorry I'm Mrs. Walker.

My apologies Mrs. Walker

As she totals and bags my items I wait for my credit card to be taken and used.

Here you go Mrs. Walker. Enjoy the rest of your stay.

Ah, I haven't paid yet.

You're not to be charged Mrs. Walker.

Excuse me, what is giving you that impression?

The resort has noted so on your account.

Then who is covering the charge?

I cannot give out that information.

But you will allow me to make charges to it?

Yes Mrs. Walker.

I'm going to kill Kevin. Can you please credit back the account and charge to this credit card *handing her my own personal – non Kevin I got this all on my own card* THANK YOU!

Leaving the shop I feel my anger building. I told this man already I do not want to be taken care of. I can buy my own damn items. Making my way back to my suite I pass the resort's outdoor cafe. Catching my eye is Kevin sitting with an older white gentleman. Who is he meeting with? He told me he was going to get a round of golf in before leaving tomorrow. Hmmm, I will see if the Hostess can tell me who he is meeting with.

Hi, I'm supposed to be meeting my husband for lunch but it seems he's meeting with someone. Before I interrupt can you tell me who he is sitting with? The table to the far right?

Are you referring to Mr. Durand?

That name again I'm referring to Mr. Walker.

Yes and he is sitting with his grandfather Mr. Durand, owner of the resort?

Excuse me?

Mrs. Walker would you like me to walk you over?

Ahem, no that won't be necessary, excuse me.

Walking as fast as my feet will allow, I head for our suite. What the hell? Wait Beth, you're on Candid Camera.... Wait for the cameras, someone will be popping out in just a second. This is a joke right? A prank? Keep waiting Beth! His grandfather? His grandfather! I know his grandparents. I met them just a few days ago in person. Spoke to both John and Adele many times before. I assumed no paternal family. He never spoke of his father and as for a paternal grandfather never. Oh and he is white??? Stop assuming Beth, Kevin will make sense of all of this. He will. I'm worrying about nothing, calm down. Remember we promised to trust again.

Arriving back to the suite I begin pacing back and forth. Stop it Beth. Pack! Yes pack, you leave in the morning. But shortly after I give myself something to do, to keep me occupied Kevin returns. Here in plain sight but with a look of you got me. This son of a bitch!

Beth I can explain

Explain what? What do you need to explain?

Beth the hostess informed me of your inquiry.

Kevin what the hell is going on? Your grandfather? Why haven't you spoke of him before?

Beth, long story.

Well glad we have all night.

No longer a deer in head lights look but rather matter closed look Beth not now.

Not now, are you kidding me? You completely left out a significant part of your life and you have nerve to say not now?

Beth not now, leave it alone.

Leave it alone…. Huh!

Why are you upset? Any other woman would be in heaven, finding out I come from money... So what the fuck..... *With deep anger in his voice* Not now Beth, please just leave it alone.

Not now.... *I begin to laugh* not NOW. Huh!
Wow! Unfortunately being told ((NOT NOW)) as if
I'm a child is an automatic trigger for me. So please
forgive me for fucking disobeying your dismissive
request.

Beth!

Kevin really? Are you kidding me? You know
everything about me. Every niche of my fucking life
presented to you even when I didn't want to share
aspects of my life, but yet you know. You know my
past, my present and damn straight you were going to
know my future because you would be a part of it.
But this, secrets why? Did you think I wasn't worthy
enough to know?

Presenting even angrier (((Most women))) is that
how you view me? Huh, so I am most women now.
Like most women I gave myself to you? Like most
women I thought you were different? But lookie here
I'm wearing a fool's cap. Thank you for allowing me
to be your court fucking jester. Thank you! *Walking
from the bedroom to the living-room, putting my flip
flops on. Kevin follows.*

Beth *in a low tone* where are you going?

41

Glancing up at Kevin, giving him a look of "don't even look my way" If I stay in this room right now I'm going to say something that I can't take back.

Beth please don't go *Kevin's voice cracking* please!

Kevin?

Beth, *Kevin with a wounded look on his face takes a seat on the sofa and gestures for me to sit aside him* I was only four when my mother passed. I didn't know about my father until I was ten. *Sighing deeply* Adele and John were my parents. They filled that void until my eighth birthday. That's when my life began to change. A strange man showed up at my grandparent's home with gift in hand. My grandmother was pissed. The first and only time I heard my grandmother swear. After about fifteen minutes of whispering, my grandparents introduced this strange man as Mr. Durand, friend of the family. From that day on I would periodically see him. But for every holiday, special occasion something big would be delivered. Bikes, go carts, ping pong table. Anything you could imagine and always the latest trend. Then during the summer of my tenth birthday it all came to ahead. My grandmother and I flew down to Texas. She said she was going to visit an old friend and thought I would like to visit with Mr. Durand. During the ride from the airport my grandmother seemed preoccupied. No words exchanged until we pulled up to this massive house. As we waited to be buzzed through the gates my grandmother stepped out of the car. Her only words were for me to mind my manners. As the car was pulling through the gate I looked back at my grandmother and saw a look I never seen before, a look I've never seen from her since.

Once at the house I was greeted by Mr. Durand. The visit was actually nice until….. Until his wife came home unexpectedly and saw me for the first time. Her stare, I will never forget it. Initially, like she saw a ghost then a look of pure anger followed by rage. She began screaming "Who allowed this bastard child into my home" Mr. Durand - grandfather tried to silence her, pulling her into another room. My curiosity got the best of me that day, following the two of them and listening outside the door. Probably the biggest mistake I ever made because I found out in that moment she – that woman was talking about me.

Seeing the pain on Kevin's face I can only imagine him as that ten year old boy. I take Kevin's hand into mine. He squeezes tightly then kisses it gently.

"My son isn't here because of that nigger girl". How dare you bring her bastard child here?

He's our grandson. We already missed years Blanche.

He is no kin to me. I will not have him in my home.

Not your home, our home and I need to make up for the horrible mistakes we made. I will have a relationship with our grandson and Blanche, if you cannot handle that I am sorry. But I can't go on like this.

Then you will be choosing that boy over me! *Raising his voice* Blanche stop it! This is exactly what you did to Jackson.

So you blame me for our son's death? Are you saying I killed my son?

Blanche you....... Blanche!

And just as that woman began to cry, a soft spoken black woman, Mrs. Clarke took me by the hand, led me into the kitchen and prepared lunch for me. Mrs. Clarke *tears in Kevin's eyes* told me I reminded her of a special boy she once knew. She spoke of him as though he was her pride and joy. She told stories of how smart and lovable he was and as the stories were told, she pulled out her bible and opened to a page marked with a picture. She removed the photograph and *tears begin to stream down Kevin's face* I saw myself. The picture of my father whom I looked like. Mrs. Clarke put the picture into my back pocket. Her words, I remember so clearly "You were made by love. Your daddy loved you and I know your mama did. They both wanted you more than life itself but sometimes life gets the best of us". *Wiping away his tears* That day I was a bit closer to knowing who I was. That day started the never ending questions.

During the flight back to Alabama I didn't say a word. My grandmother knew something was wrong. Not even a good two minutes arriving home I became unwrapped, telling my grandmother what happened. I thought she would be furious. But she wasn't. That night I learned my parents met at Texas A and M, my mother's junior year. *Smiling* Adele was surprised by her daughter's attraction to a "white boy" because of my mother's "Afrocentric views". But she was, in

45

love. Shortly after my mother graduating she found out she was expecting. My father wanted to marry her, giving her a ring *Kevin lifting my hand and kisses my engagement ring* yes this one. But when his parents found out, he was told he was making the biggest mistake of his career, of his life. My mother not wanting him to loose so much pushed him away. Last my family knew he was on one of his father's oil rigs and a massive explosion occurred in Alaska. My father and two other men were killed. As Adele explains, everyday my father was gone, a piece of life was taken from my mother. When she heard of his death, she sent me to stay with a neighbor and took an overdose. To this day my heart aches knowing I wasn't enough for her.... to live!

Kevin falls into my arms and begins to weep. My tears not only fall for him but I envision the sorrow, the pain I put Cynthia and my father through. Seeing my strong man in pieces in front of me and remembrance of my own work I too weep. But in an instant I begin pulling myself together for Kevin.

Kevin, look at me. What your mom did had nothing to do with her not loving you.

Beth don't

Listen to me... The place she was at, she probably thought what she did was to give you a better life.

Beth how can you say that?

Instantly turning my wrists over, removing my watch and bangle. I pull up my sarong that covers my thigh. All exposed now, my own embodied memorial This is how I know.

Kevin breaking down once more, burring his head into my lap.

Kevin look at me *straining to hold back my own weeping cry*

………

Wiping my own tears away ((look at me))

Looking into my eyes I've been where your mother was. *Sighing* It wasn't you. She thought she was giving you some type of happiness. It wasn't you.

Taking me into his arms, Kevin and I sit in silence. With eyes closed I continue to think about the hell I put daddy and Cynthia through. Tears begin to fall harder.

Baby I don't mean to upset you and I certainly didn't mean you were just another woman. *Sighing deeply* You're the only woman I ever wanted to be with. Before you I never experienced being in love. I knew you were the one for me the first time I laid my eyes on you.

Trying to lighten the air You did not.

Oh yes I did. Wearing a blue skirt that came to your knees, a light yellow short-sleeved blouse and blue high heel shoes.

What?

That's what you were wearing

So it was the shoes that won you over? *I begin to laugh*

No, it was your concern for Rosa and Rosie. That day I felt your hurt and pain. It was in that moment I fell in love with you.

Really Mr. Walker?

Really Mrs. Walker. *Taking my hand and displaying my ring finger* I thought this ring would remain tucked away forever. But the day my heart told me to ask you to marry me, I went out looking for the perfect ring. I couldn't find anything I thought was right. Then out of the blue I thought of my mom and the one keepsake that had meaning for both my parents, this ring *lifting my hand once again.*

Oh Kevin *kissing him gently* I hope you know how much I love you, how much I'm in love with you.

Oh I do. I just hope you can forgive me for earlier.

Forgiven

Well I think we need to get packing.

Oh not so quick Mr. Walker, how are you and your grandparents now?

I have a cordial relationship with my grandfather and Blanche – nothing. Over the years my grandfather has tried his best to make up for any wrong. He paid for my education, purchased my first car. He's given me the opportunity to travel, often with him to Africa, the Gulf and many parts of Europe s*miling* his way of introducing me to his business.

Kevin how did you end up being a New Yorker?

Well, I became a bit much for Adele and John. Back then I didn't understand the rejection, my mother, I didn't understand my life. My lack of understanding turned into disobeying my grandparents, drinking, not coming home etc. My grandfather offered to put me into military school, paying all expenses but you met my grandmother,

Adele was not having that. So my uncle who was a detective here in NY came to Alabama packed my things and told me I had no choice. And if I needed convincing his kicking my ass would provide any missing information to help me understand. It was a difficult transition at first, but after a few months with my Uncle I changed and began getting my life back on track. He saved my life.

Why haven't I met him?

During my senior year at Colgate he was killed by a drug dealer in Brooklyn.

Oh Kevin....

I was certain Adele was going to break, both her children taken away so tragically. But no, she made it. However I just about gave her a heart attack when I entered the Police Academy. The one area both she and JD - grandfather agreed on, continuing my education and not becoming a cop. JD wanted me to continue at Harvard for my MBA but instead I went to Columbia and obtained my Masters in Forensic Psychology. Year to date he hasn't given up. He believes I should be his successor, take over for him but that life, not for me.

Your father didn't have any siblings?

No. I guess that's why he had such a need to establish a relationship with me. The only heir.

Other than owning this hotel *giving Kevin my disapproval look from earlier today* what does your grandfather's company do?

Beth you really never heard of Durand Holdings?

Ah no. Should I know the name?

Beth Durand Oil?

No... Sorry?

Laughing Beth you really didn't and don't know who I am?

Know who you are? Strange question. I know you as Kevin Jackson Walker, my husband.

Still laughing baby that is who I am.

Kevin, why don't you have your father's name?

Beth I have it, I don't use it.

Why?

Because of what I do. Because of my grandfather's worth, only a handful of people know who I am and who I am related to. *Looking me straight in the eyes* Beth for your safety I need you to keep this to yourself.

What is there to share, I never heard of him and Kevin is probably exaggerating the wealth? I will...

But one last question.... Why is your grandfather here?

I called him for help?

Help? Help with what?

Beth...... with you?

Excuse me? *Not sure how I should feel about his reply*

I should have told you this sooner.

Told me what?

Lowering his head as if he is ashamed Karen Morris was found dead several weeks ago

Kevin as sad as this news is I'm sort of relieved. I feel bad for her girls but

Interrupting me ((Beth))

Kevin?

Beth she died almost a year ago.

What? No impossible

She wasn't the person who ......

Immediately standing to my feet Kevin that can't be, she that woman.... It was her.

The medical examiner in North Carolina confirmed Beth, it wasn't her.

How did she die?

She was murdered, an overdose of heroine.

Then that means… *Shaking uncontrollably my mind begins to wonder who could be behind this and why?* Okay but Kevin, things have been quiet. It's been months since….

Beth, *Kevin's voice almost a whisper* my apartment building, a fire at my building two days ago.

Oh My God, was anyone hurt?

No… The Fire Department's preliminary findings point to arson.

Holding my hands to my face Kevin how can this be?

Beth I don't know.

Also my car was vandalized while parked in the lot at the airport.

Could that be just a coincidence?

Beth please I need you to take this for what it is. Someone is out to harm you. I thought keeping this information from you would be best but I was wrong. You must take this seriously.

Kevin *tears begin trickling down my face* I just…… I don't understand why!

Baby, *sighing deeply* I will find out who is behind this…

Kevin words send a cold chill down my back... I recall the words said to me when I was abducted "You're lucky nothing is going on between you and that detective because he would have been next". I begin to cry uncontrollably.

Baby I will do everything to keep you safe.

Trying to control my crying but now I've put you in danger!

Beth, I'm a big boy *and Kevin chuckles* I can take care of myself. How many times do I need to tell you that? But you on the other hand, as hardheaded as you are, you're my first and only priority. *Kevin takes me into his arms and holds me ever so tightly.*

Composing myself Okay then what's the plan?

To start, we will be staying at my grandfather's home in the Hamptons.

The Hampton's Kevin? So far!

Beth!

Alright the Hamptons. But I will be returning to work on Monday. I'm not backing down on this.

You do recall me saying you did not need to work?

Do you recall me saying I did not want you taking care of me financially?

Your one stubborn woman!

And that's one of the things you love about me.

Hmmm

Alrighty then, let's get this packing thing under way. Oh and one more thing Mr. Walker finding out your bi-racial *with a straight face* Kevin your nationality, dual race that's a problem.... I don't do white guys!

Forcefully pulling me into his arms too bad baby... You have me for life!

Chapter Four – Hello and You Are?

How are you feeling?

Kevin, I was a bit excited when you told me we were flying back privately but I never expected this *who am I trying to fool, I thought when you said a small private plane, it would be a small twenty seater where the passengers and cockpit crew were separated by a curtain. Not this.*

Sorry if this is uncomfortable for you, my grandfather's idea.

No Kevin I feel swell flying in your grandfather's private plane wearing my no name jeans, jewelry purchased from the spot on Jamaica Avenue – The Coliseum and last but not least my wanna be Gucci pocketbook purchased from one of my favorite Chinese vendors on Main Street in Flushing. Yup, feeling mighty pretty right now. No not uncomfortable *please God no lightning strikes.*

Mr. and Mrs. Walker can I offer you a cocktail?

I'll have a water, Beth what would you like?

A barf bag please. Oh if this is how the wealthy travels thank God I'm not. Why do I feel every bump? Could I have a vodka with orange juice?

Sure Mrs. Walker

As the stewardess walks away Beth are you sure about the vodka? You look a little green right now.

Kevin not funny. I'm hoping the vodka will put me out. This flight isn't exactly agreeing with me.

Here you go Mrs. Walker. Can I get you anything else?

No I think my motion sickness is out of your control.

Smiling But I could provide you with a cool compress?

No I will be fine but thank you.

Could you give us a pillow and a blanket?

Sure Mr. Walker

Oh my God, what is she thinking we need a pillow and blanket for? Whispering Kevin why do you want a pillow and a blanket?

Kevin with an ever so large smile on his face Get your mind out of the gutter Mrs. Walker. The pillow and the blanket are for you. I know how you get after one drink. Just getting prepared!

Feeling very foolish Oh *laughing*

Here you are Mr. Walker

Thank you

Kevin are we still flying into JFK?

Yes. Erickson and a security detail will meet us.

A security detail, is that really necessary?

And you were doing so well not fighting me on this.

I just find it….. Forget it *and I yawn*

That drink kicking in huh….

Funny!

Then that long drive. Kevin are you sure you want to drive all the way to the Hamptons? In the snow?

Yes I do and we are.

Taking the pillow and placing it across Kevin's lap Let me know when we land.

Kevin brushing my hair with his hand Beth I wish you would consider delaying your return to work.

In my sleepy voice I would if I could but I can't so I won't *laughing at my own response Kevin slaps my behind softly* Will you be returning to work tomorrow Mr. Walker or are you considering delaying your return?

Beth go to sleep *and I am kissed on the forehead.*

I awake from my nap by the stewardess informing Kevin and I of our arrival at JFK. The temperature is a warm 26 degrees and it is snowing.

Mr. and Mrs. Walker welcome back to New York - J.F.K. International Airport. The time is now 4:28 p.m.

After pulling into a private hanger, the captain comes out from the cockpit. Kevin I didn't realize it was you onboard until the tower just now inquiring. How are you?

Wow Devlin, how are you? *The two exchange pleasantries then somewhat of a bro hug.*

How's the family?

Everyone is well.

And you?

Well, let me introduce you to my beautiful wife, Beth

Nice to meet you Devlin

Nice to meet you Mrs. Walker *looking at Kevin with an awkward smile. Yep must be the no name jeans.*

So your grandfather's resort, the honeymoon? I hope the two of you enjoyed!

We did

Well nice to meet you Mrs. Walker

Nice to meet you as well

As Kevin and I begin exiting the plane into the that warm twenty-six degree weather a dark colored SUV pulls up to the plane along with a familiar car. Stepping out of the SUV, two men dressed in dark colored suits. The familiar car, Erickson.

Beth did you enjoy your honeymoon *Ericson asks as he kisses me on the cheek.*

It was absolutely wonderful.

Hey man good trip? *Ericson asking Kevin.*

Yes it was. *Kevin presenting business like, no longer presenting as a honeymooner or vacationer but rather a man consumed with worry and concern. As Kevin and Ericson continue what seems to be a one sided conversation another vehicle pulls up. Kevin takes me by the hand and walks over to the vehicle as an older gentleman steps out.*

Good evening Charles. Thank you for meeting us on such short notice

Of course and you must be the newly Mrs. Walker.

Yes I am. Nice to meet you Charles *even though I have no idea as to who you are.*

Beth Charles is the head of my grandfather's security. *Gesturing now for me to get into the vehicle*

Charles came out of I need to speak with Charles and Ericson for a few minutes *closing the door behind me.*

Approximately ten minutes and a lot of hand gesturing later Kevin joins me in the back seat. Charles now in the passenger seat and one of the two unknown gentleman in the driver's seat. Driving in front of us the second half of the two unknown gentleman and behind us, Erickson.

Kevin continuing to sport the same look since landing back in New York, the same look from the night of our wedding, a look that is completely consuming him right now.

Hey everything okay?

Grasping my hand it is Beth.

Then why the worried look?

No worries I promise

Unable to control my curiosity, leaning into Kevin are you uncomfortable with me meeting your grandfather?

Baby is that what you think?

Based on yesterday, yes. Kevin clearly our social statuses are on two different levels.

Beth you're my wife and I can't help but to show you off so if you think I am ashamed to have you, be around you... Baby never in a million years

But yesterday

Interrupting Beth yesterday was all me. This will be the first time my grandfather.... Beth letting my grandfather into my life, this is a first. The anger wasn't at you but myself.

Love, if you're not sure you want to pursue a relationship right now slow it down. I'm sure he will understand.

Beth so many emotions and for the first time in my life I'm happy. If you haven't picked up on it, I'm a closed book. But page by page you.... Thanks to you I'm allowing others in a bit more. To allow my grandfather in but at a distance.

Kevin that isn't a bad thing

I know baby...... Now, when are we going to start house hunting?

First, I think we need to agree on an area!

Well what's your pleasure Long Island or upstate?

Are you kidding? Why so far? I was thinking along the lines of Queens!

Hmmm, next weekend we could take a casual ride up to Westchester and Rockland just to see what's around.

I see you already have a preference!

No not really. But will you take the drive with me?

Foolish question, of course I will

Still feeling the effects of my one vodka drink, I lay my head against his shoulder. Kevin wraps his arms round me.

Better?

Much....

With this snow we still have about an hour on the road, rest and I will wake you when we arrive.

Yawning I whisper This is what happens when you spend a week doing literarily nothing but *turning my head to look Kevin in the eyes* hopping like rabbits *and I bust out laughing.*

Laughing Beth please remind me to lock up the alcohol. Now go to sleep.

Taking my husband's advice I close my eyes. Kevin stroking my back I find myself drifting into a soft restful slumber.

About an hour later I'm awakened by Kevin
Beth...... Beth

Are we here? *And before Kevin answers I feel the cold air forcefully hitting me. The passage side door opens and I am face to face with an older white gentleman with a heavy southern accent.*

Well how are you?

Well thank you *looking up at Kevin.*

Extending his hand to help me out the SUV, Kevin behind me guiding by way of my waist. Grandfather I would like you to meet my wife, Beth.

So you're the special someone!

That's what he claims but I'm sure if Halle Berry strolled by I would be forgotten about in a second.

With a bellowing laughing response, Kevin shakes his head at me then smiles.

Beautiful and a sense of humor.

Why thank you sir.

If you too are done, let's get inside *Kevin along with Charles taking our luggage from the car. He motions to Erickson and the two unknown gentlemen to follow*

Entering the grand foyer I am stunned by the absolute beauty of the home. You have a beautiful home Mr. Durand.

Please call me JD and this is your home also, you and my grandson's.

Grandfather thank you but no we…..

Son this is your home and you can stay here for as long as you want. But your grandmother and I would like to get you two something maybe in Manhattan as a wedding present. That Long Island Expressway is a beast

Interrupting ((Grandfather)) I appreciate the gesture but allowing Beth and I to stay here for now is all that is needed.

Well son whatever you want… I'm here

As Kevin and his grandfather whom I never knew existed until yesterday continues their strange exchanges an older black woman enters and bear hugs Kevin. Kevin's facial expression completely changes, sporting now a very large smile.

Mrs. Clarke I did not know you were here. *Kevin now twirling her around.*

So this is Mrs. Clarke. If not understanding why he is so thrilled to see her I would be a bit jealous right now.

Another heavy southern accent Your granddaddy told me he was coming to see you and I jumped at the chance to see my baby boy. But a baby boy you are not. How are you?

Well and even better since marrying this beautiful woman. I would like you to meet my wife Elizabeth Walker.

Well beautiful you are sweetheart *and I am bear hugged.*

Nice to meet you

I made the master suite up for you two. Why don't you two get settled in, supper will be ready in about an hour.

That sounds great Mrs. Clarke. I'll take Beth up. Grandfather could we meet in the study in about fifteen minutes?

Certainly, son! You two get settled and I will talk to these fine men *eyeing Kevin as if he knew what the topic was going to be.*

Leading the way, Kevin caresses my hand as we walk up the grand stairway. Once on the upper level we pass at least five bedrooms ending at the end of a massive hallway. When the double doors are opened, I am completely blown away. A massive bedroom with one complete wall of floor to ceiling windows and French doors that overlook the beach. During the summer this must be a fantastic view because it certainly isn't bad in January. But as I continue my sweep of the room I find Kevin sitting on the side of the bed with his hands covering his face. Grasping his face to look up at me Mr. Walker are you okay?

I am Beth... I think the day is catching up with me.

Hey *sitting next to him* what can I do to make it better?

You already are, being here!

Your grandfather seems like a hoot?

Hmmm

Hmmm what?

Just that I love you... So I'm going to head down and talk to Erickson. You should give Cynthia a call and let her know what the plan is.

Ok but first, *pushing Kevin down onto the bed and climbing on top of him* promise me dinner will be quick so we can *I begin kissing Kevin, first touching his face then making my way down his front, ending at his manhood which is already alert. Climbing off him Kevin grabs my hips and positions me back on him.*

Mr. Walker we can't right now!

Ignoring me my shirt is being pulled over my head. Beth they can wait.

No they can't. But I promise after dinner, just you and me.

I'm going to keep you at your word.

Please do because I will be keeping myself at my own word *and I laugh.*

Kevin heads downstairs and I adhere to Kevin's suggestion, Calling Cynthia. Taking my cell out, four missed calls. First from Adele and John making sure we were back. Two messages from Cynthia wondering where we are and the last from Rochelle just saying hello and hoping we could talk before Monday. I'll call Cynthia first.

Hello?

Oh Mrs. Walker

No its Beth… Ms. Walker if you're nasty *and I begin to laugh*

Your one sick chick. How was the honeymoon

Oh Cynthia it was absolutely perfect.

So when am I going to see you and better yet when are you picking up this psychotic cat?

Oh my Tiger!

Tiger my ass. He has broken and clawed his way around my house.

Laughing He was only expressing his love for you Cynthia.

Beth…

Still laughing sorry!

But on a serious note everything okay?

The same old stuff.

Well a few things I need to share with you.

What happened?

To start Kevin and I are staying at his grandfather's home

You're in Alabama???

Long story but no, his paternal grandfather.

Huh?

Yup…

So he has paternal grandparents. Why weren't they at the wedding?

Cynthia, a conversation to be had in person with a large pot of tea!

That bad huh?

Not bad or good, just *sighing* …. A topic for another day.

Where are you now?

Out in the Hamptons!

Beth does this have anything to do with Karen? Did anything happen?

Well to start she was killed almost a year ago.

Beth I'm already aware of that. Did anything happen? *The sound of concern in her voice.*

How do you know that?

Kevin… The day of the wedding.

Unsure how I should feel about this, discussing with Cynthia instead of me?

Beth?

………

Beth I know you're not stewing over Kevin discussing this with me. He wanted you to have a remarkable evening and you did!

Cynthia you're missing the point.

No Beth you are. Get over it!

Anyway

((Anyway)) did something happen?

While we were away Kevin's apartment building caught fire, believed to be arson.

Anyone harmed?

Thank God no. But that's not all. The car was vandalized while parked at the airport.

Okay so you will not put up a fight, you will not give Kevin a hard time and you will do what you are told!

Cynthia?

Shrieking ((Beth)) *Just as Cynthia is about to begin telling me off, Kevin enters and puts his arms around me.*

Cynthia I'm being accosted by a very handsome but strange man.

Hey Kevin… *Cynthia yells*

Hi Cynt

Cynthia let me call you back.

Make sure you do. ((Talk to you later Kevin))

((I will make sure she calls you back))

I hang up with Cynthia. Kevin takes a seat on the lounger and motions me to sit on his lap.

So did you and Erickson take care of whatever needed to be taken care of?

It depends?

Depends on what?

You!

Why me?

Well because you have great difficulty following directions.

And what direction do you want me to adhere to?

Delay returning to work!

Nope… Next

I knew that would be your response.

Oh you know me so well *I kiss Kevin on the lips.*

Starting Monday you will be chauffeured to and from work. While at work you will have security with you.

Standing now in front of Kevin I retract what I just said, obviously you don't know me as well as I thought you did!

Beth you think this is open for negotiations? I apologize if I gave you that impression. Case closed!

Kevin not ha…

((BETH, CASE CLOSED) *A look of pure anger on his face*

What about you?

What about me?

Who has your back?

Softening his voice Baby I have my own back. You're the focus not me.

So you're going in tomorrow?

Yes Beth and I will be just fine. Grandfather will be here until Tuesday. Charles will stay back until everything is straight with the security details. Grandfather upgraded the security both here and the detail going into the city with you. Mrs. Clarke will remain during our stay.

Kevin...... Forget it....

Beth this is for your protection. I'm not backing down from this.

But I need to gather items from my apartment. I need clothes for work!

Already covered! Tomorrow Erickson and I will go and check on both apartments. I will pack your things for work.

Couldn't I just do it?

NO!

Whatever...

Caressing my behind, Really Mr. Walker?

What??

Hmmm

Kissing me Let's go down for dinner. If I recall correctly you and I have a date.

A smile reemerges upon my face Yes we do.

Chapter Five – Have We Met Before?

Waking from an unsettled sleep I look over at the clock on the nightstand, 4:30 in the morning. The alarm will be going off in a half an hour. I lay here in bed worrying about how I'm going to spend my day without Kevin. I don't know Mrs. Clarke nor JD. They both seem like lovely people but..... How can I occupy myself for the next twelve to fourteen hours? I need to shop but Kevin will probably have a problem with that. Smiling he will get over it. I'll mention it as he dresses for work.

Getting up as gently as possible, I go down to the kitchen and put on the kettle. I'm in total awe of this massive kitchen, absolutely beautiful. Scanning the counter I find the coffee maker. Going through the cabinets, coffee and tea found. As the coffee begins to brew I grab two slices of bread and put them in the toaster. Taking about twenty minutes to prepare, all is done now. Finding a beautiful tray, I place all items on it and head back to our room. Looking at the clock Kevin still has about ten minutes. I'll go into the bathroom and at least wash my face and brush my teeth.

Tasks completed. Exiting the bathroom I'm startled. Kevin already awake, sitting on the lounger sipping his coffee.

Baby I'm sorry I woke you.

With a devilish smile Come here....

Knowing what is on his mind I walk over and sit on Kevin's lap Mr. Walker I know where this is going and you have no time.

What *smiling* I just wanted to thank you for this *pointing to the tray* and to say good morning.

Hearing good morning isn't the part that worries me.

No worries baby *and I am kissed passionately. Any hesitations I had are replaced with my immediate disrobing and taking seat directly onto Kevin, facing him. Immediately my body reacts and I find myself grinding forcefully. Kevin knowing what my need is, grasps my hips, allowing his hands to act like anchors as he thrust upwards. The sensation so pleasing, I reach my peak, calling out Kevin's name. My acknowledgment of Kevin activates his need to release, and in an instant I am filled with a reward. Holding me tightly, I look into my husband's face and kiss him with all my love.*

Good morning Mrs. Walker

Good morning Mr. Walker, I love your early morning greetings.

And I love you. Beth thanks for this *picking up a slice of toast and positioning it near my mouth for me to take a bite.*

Your welcome *pulling my self-off of Kevin and onto my feet*

Beth I want you to feel comfortable here today. Mrs. Clarke and Charles will get you whatever you want or need.

Kevin you know that isn't going to mesh well with me. But I will be fine. *Here I go* I do plan on going out to do some shopping.

Kevin looking at me with sort of a disapproval look And where do you plan on going to?

Get ready, brace yourself Probably Queens to Jamaica or Green Acres Mall!

Smiling, Beth I will make a deal with you

This isn't going to be good, go ahead

I can agree with you doing some shopping but

I knew it but what?

Listen to me... No Jamaica Avenue or Green Acres.

Then where?

East Hampton Mall

Kevin, did I not review my salary with you? I can't shop there.

Laughing, Beth two days ago you found out you're a wealthy woman.

No a few days ago I found out my husband is an heir to a wealthy empire, has nothing to do with me.

No longer a smile on his face. If you want to shop it has to be here in the Hamptons. The two credit cards I gave you have no limits. You can afford to shop at.......

Interrupting with attitude Kevin I...

Beth that is it! Traveling to Queens isn't going to happen. Thomas and Donaldson will drive you to and from, be with you in the stores etc. *Raised tone* Do not attempt to convince them to do anything other than my instructions. Do you understand? I will be pissed Beth! This is not a joke!

Here I go again, getting turned on by this man when he is all riled up.... Kevin alright!

Okay Beth, *walking over to me* baby your safety is my only priority *and I'm kissed on the lips.*

77

While Kevin showers I make the bed. I begin pulling clothing from our luggage, sorting what needs to be washed and what needs to be put away. By the time I'm done, Kevin is out the shower and dressed.

Beth what are you doing?

What?

You don't need to make the bed or do laundry.

Listen, this is who I am. I can take care of myself.....

Yes you can. No one doubts that. The issue however is with the decisions you make!

Ha ha... very funny.

Hmmm alright baby I am out of here. I will call and check in with you.

Don't worry about me. Obviously you are leaving me in good hands. Better yet I have a feeling you have a way of checking in on me.

With a devilish look, oh I do....

Whatever.... *Looking into my husband's eyes* I love you soo much Mr. Walker.

And I love you Mrs. Walker. *One last kiss and a swat on my bottom, Kevin leaves for work.*

Taking note of the time 5:35 a.m. I decide to get a handle on the laundry, the pressing need - no clean underwear. I jump into the shower for a few minutes and dress only in my robe. Trying to hold as much as I can in my arms I go down to the kitchen. I laugh to myself, where in the hell would the laundry area be? Dropping the items on the floor, I'm halted in place by JD standing in front of me. My reaction in the form of a squeaky yell.

Beth are you okay?

I'm soo sorry, I was looking for the laundry room.

Just leave it right there, Mrs. Clarke will take care of it.

No I would rather do it myself. Do you have any idea where the washer is?

I think behind one of these doors, *walking to each, opening the first door,* no this is the pantry. *Second door,* here it is.

Great thank you. *I pick up my items as quickly as possible, embarrassed by all my undergarments being on display. Coming out of the laundry room about five minutes later I find JD sitting at the table. He looks as if he is testing his sugar but not succeeding?*

Hey let me help you with that *holding his shaking hands, I hold one and guide the other with the needle.*

Thank you Beth. The older these old eyes get the harder it is for me to do this.

No problem. But did you eat anything yet?

No I didn't want to wake Mrs. Clarke. But why are you up Beth?

Standing now, looking through the refrigerator I got up with Kevin. How about an egg omelet with tomatoes?

Beth I don't want you to go through the trouble

No trouble *and I begin pulling items from the refrigerator*

Kevin said you are staying until Tuesday?

Yes then I'm heading to West Africa.

Wow... business or pleasure?

Business... Moments like this and last night are my pleasure. Beth my grandson is the happiest I have ever seen him and I need to thank you for that.

Please no thanks... Kevin fills me with happiness as well. Would you like a little cheese?

Yes cheese sounds divine.

Pulling a plate and glass from the cupboard and silverware from the drawer I set all items in front of

JD. As I plate I see JD with a worried look on his face. I take a seat across from him.

JD are you okay?

Beth I am *Tears forming in his eyes* I'm just an old man fortunate enough to meet my grandson's wife.

Oh JD, I'm glad I met you too and old.... Not a day over 40.

Laughing your too kind. Come this October I will be the big 72...

Really? You don't look like a man of 72...

Well thank you.

How would you like your coffee?

Milk and sugar...

I can do the low fat milk but the sugar?????

I thought I would try *with a childlike smile on his face* I will take it with the low fat milk. So I assume Kevin told you the plan for tomorrow?

Yes he did... *Looking a bit annoyed*

Beth you will be fine, my security team is one of the best.

JD I'm sure they are, I just think it is silly. Your grandson is over reacting.

No I think he's right on top of it. This isn't anything to take lightly.

Oh not him too I guess JD

It is none of my business but you don't have to return to work right now!

I must be in a time warp, have I not already heard these same words? I see you and your grandson have similar views. JD I don't know if Kevin told you but up to a few days ago I didn't know who you were and certainly didn't know Kevin's wealth. With that said, since finding out my finances remain the same. I work not only to put food on the table but also because I like what I do. Going to work isn't an option and I will be going in tomorrow.

Under different circumstances I would agree but

Interrupting no but JD, this is something I must do. Besides I'm going back with a new title, Director.

Well congratulations darling.

Thank you *I begin clearing the table*

Beth leave them, Mrs. Clarke will take care of it.

No, a habit I must clean up after myself *and I smile*

Well Beth thank you for a delicious breakfast. This old man is going to dress and take a walk.

Would you like some company?

I would love the company

Great! I will meet you back here in a half an hour? Perfect!

After tidying up the kitchen and dressing JD and I meet as planned and begin our walk.

So do you always travel with an entourage?
Referring to the security bunch following us.

Unfortunately Beth I have to and now you do as well.

I'm sure this thing whatever it is will be over soon. But enough about that how often do you stay here in the Hamptons?

I purchased this house when Kevin moved to New York. I'm a true southern boy so coming to New York wasn't a priority until he moved here. Since, I try to spend as much time as I can here. Usually at least one or two weekends a month.

So in Texas, I will assume a large cattle ranch?

Laughing not all Texan's have a ranch but yes this old boy, I do. I grew up working on a ranch, my daddy was a ranch hand for many years.

Please forgive me if I'm prying but you weren't wealthy growing up?

No no no. Not at all. My daddy was a ranch hand and my mama a domestic.

Then how did you become this very wealthy oilman?

While in the army I purchased a deed to some land in Texas. Turned out crude oil - pure gold was found on the property. From that I ventured into off shore drilling etc.

Wow

Stopping and looking me in the eyes that's why Beth I respect your decision to work during what is going on. Not too many of us around with a dedicated work ethic. But at the same time I don't want to see my grandson worry.

Taking JD's hand into mine, you really love your grandson!

I do. I made so many mistakes with my son which affected Kevin. I'm just trying to make up for time loss.

JD we all have made mistakes, part of our human makeup. We can't change the past but we can prevent making the same mistakes in our present and future.

Kissing my hand Thank you Beth. *Looking down at his watch* by now the bakery should be open, do you mind if we walk in that direction.

We can but I will be eyeing what you get.

I had a feeling you would *and we laugh.*

Already four in the afternoon I return from my non - productive – non shopping spree with Willy and Wonka. Not one word exchanged between us. Only doors open and closed for me and being followed. I sit here panicking a bit. What am I going to wear tomorrow? I hope whatever Kevin obtains from my apartment is appropriate for tomorrow. Interrupting my thoughts, my cell is ringing.

Hello

Mrs. Walker, how did the shopping go?

Oh it went

What do you mean by "it went"?

Nothing... How's your day going?

Beth the shopping, did you get anything?

………..

Beth?

I couldn't find anything in my price range Mr. Walker!

((Beth))

Kevin not open for discussion. What time will you be back at the house?

About seven. Erickson and I will stop by the apartments first.

Okay... Can you remember work attire for me?

You wouldn't need to worry about your attire if you wasn't so stubborn.

Whatever Mr. Walker.... I love you and will see you later.

Love you Mrs. Walker.

Just as I end my call with Kevin, a knock at the door. Come in

Mrs. Walker here are your things

Mrs. Clarke please call me Beth

Okay Beth and you can leave your laundry in the basket in the bathroom and I will take care of it.

Thank you *feeling a bit uncomfortable*

Beth I will be preparing supper, anything in particular you would like?

No Mrs. Clarke, anything you prepare I'm sure will be great but can I help?

No I have it. Besides I was told you would be returning to work tomorrow. Take this time and prepare. Enjoy the last few hours of your vacation.

I guess *sensing my boredom and seeing the look of disappointment on my face*

You know Beth I could use some help. When you're done up here come on down and we will prepare supper together.

Smiling I would like that a lot Mrs. Clarke, Thank you.

Chapter Six – Calling All Directors

My first day back to work after months of working from home. I feel like a child on the first day of school after a long summer's break. I just wish I wasn't traveling with Frick and Frat. I would love to be in the front seat of this beautiful fully loaded beamer with music pumping. I can only imagine how Elvis would sound pumping through the speakers. Better yet the mood I'm in, a little Santana and Rob Thomas singing Smooth. But nope I'm in the backseat twiddling my thumbs. Putting my headset on I begin listening to Santana.

About fifteen minutes into my private music session I open my eyes to Laurel or is it Hardy saying something to me. Lips moving but I can't hear. Giggling to myself, maybe if I remove the ear phones communication would occur.

Sorry had my music on

Ma'am Mr. Walker would like to speak with you. He ask that you answer your phone.

Pulling my phone out of my purse, yup he's a calling Hello Mr. Walker

Mrs. Walker, do you think it is wise to play your music so loud? So loud you can't hear your phone or hear someone in the same car talking to you?

Lowering my voice Mr. Walker I hear Moe and Curly just fine. Are we in a bad mood?

No not at all. Just stating the facts!

How can I help you Mr. Walker?

Just confirming you were on the road and to remind you of the rules.

Kevin!

BETH!

Laughing Yes I remember the rules. No communication with anyone regarding the investigation.

I mean no one Beth!

I know, I get it.

Okay…. I will check in with you later and "Donaldson and Thomas" will be with you throughout the day. A vacant office on the same floor has been rented and security along with "Donaldson and Thomas" will be housed.

I guess his repeat of Donaldson and Thomas is Kevin's way of confirming the two have actual names. You have too much time on your hands.

Beth don't start!

I'm not, just saying. I will keep to the plan!

Thank you!

Alright baby get back to work. I will check in with you later today.

Love you!

Arriving to the office around eight fort-five, Donaldson yes I think he's Donaldson and I are dropped off right in front of the building. Escorted to the seventeenth floor, I'm shown where security is housed. I can't believe Kevin and his grandfather, renting a complete office suite? I should have figured the command post is literally right next door. Ridiculous!

Good Morning Paige

Good Morning Beth… Wow you look wonderful. Married life fits you *kissing me on my cheek*

Thank you *blushing* Where can I find Rochelle?

In your office

In my office *sounding a bit confused*

Yes she's waiting for you

Oh… Okay *walking toward my office*

Beth?

Yes Paige?

Where are you going?

Paige to my office!

You do know your office is the other way?

No it isn't... *and I continue to walk down the hall. Opening the door I am startled by a young woman sitting at my desk.*

Good Morning can I help you?

Umm this is my office

Oh you must be Mrs. Morris?

Actually Mrs. Walker. You are?

Just then Rochelle and Paige are standing in the doorway giggling. I see you met your newest hire, Daphne Moore.

Smiling Hello Daphne so sorry.

Rochelle interrupting Beth is the new director I told you about.

Extending her hand we shake

How do you like working here so far?

I love it

Great...

Catching me looking around my office You have a lot of drawings from Rosie. Your daughter?

Ahem... No just someone very dear to me.

Rochelle noticing the pain surfacing upon my face
Beth can we go down to your office now?

Sure, Daphne we can talk some more a bit later.

I would like that

Following Rochelle to her office, rather my office neither of us take seat behind the desk but at the round table.

So Mrs. Walker how was the trip?

Rochelle absolutely wonderful. Couldn't ask for anything more. What about you, how are the girls?

Everyone is great especially since the arrival of our new addition to the Horowitz clan.

What????

Laughing The puppy Lindsay received over the holidays.

Oh, what type of puppy is he or she?

A male Pekinese named Tinker.

Tinker?

That's the name Lindsay came up with *pulling a picture out of her purse*

He's adorable

Back to you Beth, any new information regarding the …..You know the incident?

Still no arrest. *I hear Kevin's voice "Do not discuss this case with anyone"* But I'm hopeful! *Changing the subject as quickly as I can* So what time do you need to head over to the Mayor's office?

Looking down at her watch About now. I just wanted to make sure you were settled in.

Pulling a small box from my purse nothing big but this is for you.

Opening the box a smile emerges upon Rochelle's face Beth you shouldn't have but I love it.

Listen I don't know if I ever said thank you for hiring a young naive girl who needed a lot, I mean a lot of guidance.

No you never thanked me and for good reason, it wasn't necessary.

Rochelle I will miss you greatly

Interrupted Stop! You and I will see each other. I'm only a few blocks away. Matter of fact let's do lunch next week.

You got it. *Rochelle now to her feet, I stand and hug Rochelle tightly* Good luck… and I already look forward to next week.

Rochelle leaves without looking back. Probably for the same reason I couldn't look up. Tears in both our eyes. Composing myself I sit back down in Rochelle's chair, correction officially now my chair. Sitting here in the midst of reality, my responsibilities as director unnerves me. I'm not going to sit here and convince myself I can't do this because I know I can. I just need time to adjust. Taking out my note pad and pen I begin compiling a do list.

Knock.... Knock...

Come in

Beth these just came for you

On my how beautiful! Thank you Paige!

Returning to my list

Beth you're not going to look at the card, to see who sent them?

It can only be my loving husband but to end your inquisitiveness I will take a look. *Pulling out the card and reviewing it I am pleasantly surprised. Not from Kevin but his grandfather.*

Sporting a large grin Are they from Kevin?

Still smiling, no from his grandfather.

Wow is he rich?

Huh..... What in the world would give you that impression?

The type of lilies they are. I'm in the middle of planning my wedding and these *pointing to the vase* were way out of my price range.

So what have I missed around here? *Changing the subject!*

It's been quiet.

How was your holiday?

It was great.

Was Santa good to you?

Laughing Not as good as he was to you *eyeing my wedding rings*. But he was nice *holding up her ring finger.*

Paige, absolutely beautiful.

Thank you. Oh did you receive your invitation yet?

Not yet. We just got back late Saturday and haven't had a chance yet to review the mail.

Please tell me you will come!

Of course I will be attending.

Great!

Paige before you go can we review what needs to be accomplished during this week?

Sure I'll just grab my pad.

Just as Paige leaves my office my phone rings
Beth Walker

Good Morning Mrs. Walker

An immediate smile surfaces upon my face.
Whispering I'm sorry, please do not call me again my husband will not understand!

Not funny Beth!

Laughing Hi my love

How is everything?

So far, so good. How is your day going?

Fine.... How was the drive in?

Mutt and Jeff were fine. You do know I prefer to drive myself?

Yes I do Beth and I doubt you will let me forget it.

A little pissed by the comment What can I do for your Mr. Walker?

Just checking in and to insure no field activity was scheduled for today!

Don't worry about me Mr. Walker. I will be in the office the entire day. Now you get back to work. I love you and will see you this evening.

Bye love...

Paige lurking in my doorway Come on in Paige. Okay, I would like to setup a department meeting for tomorrow at ten. Anyone with appointments unless extremely urgent should reschedule.

Okay

Everyone should come prepared with a list of their current cases and status of each.

Okay

Has Daphne shadowed anyone yet?

No, Rochelle wanted her to become familiar with policy first.

Great. Okay that should be it for now.

Walking out of my office with Paige I walk to my old office.

Knock....... Knock

Come in

Hi Daphne I was hoping we could meet for a few minutes?

Sure Beth

Taking a seat I begin to scan my office for my personal belongings. Can you tell me where my personal items are?

Rochelle packed your items. If not mistaken you should find the boxes in your office?

Smiling Just so thrilled to be back I didn't notice. So Daphne can you tell me a little about yourself?

I'm currently attending Hunter College, working on my Master's in Social Work.

What field of Social Work do you plan to get into?

Probably mental health – counseling.

What brought you here to Care House?

One of my professor's suggested Care House, Amanda Barnes?

Amanda, yes she is one of the board members.

Professor Barnes knew I was looking for a job and of course knew I needed to begin my internship. She felt I could do both through Care House.

Well great. How do you like being here so far?

Everyone has been great. I look forward to doing field work.

Good. I'm going to pair you up with Pam. Have you met Pam yet?

Not sure

I'll do a formal introduction tomorrow. The department will be meeting at 10. Until then continue to review the policy and procedure manual. I will also pull a few charts for you to review and become familiar with.

Thank you Beth.

Returning to my office I review my to do list as well as my schedule for tomorrow. By the time I'm done my watch reads 4:50 p.m.

Knock…. Knock……

Come in

Beth a gentleman is here to see you

Must be either Heckle or Jeckle Paige just have him take a seat and I will be out in a moment. You go on home and I will see you in the morning.

With a very large smile, Beth are you sure?

About you going home, absolutely. I will close up.

No I meant about the person waiting for you?

Yes I'm sure. He can wait a few minutes

In that moment, I hear "I can" *and standing in front of me is my husband.*

What the heck are you doing here?

To take you home

Paige lingering about, Paige you can go, I will lockup. And thank you for today.

You are welcome Beth. Have a good evening Detective Walker *Paige says with an extremely large smile on her face.*

Paige leaves my office, closing the door behind herself. I stand and walk directly to my husband and kiss him hard.

Beth stop that! You know what that does to me.

I know, that's why I do it. Now what are you doing here?

I thought I would relieve you from Frick and Frack or is it Mutt and Jeff?

Ha ha very funny. But I'm glad you're here. *Packing up my bag, I notice Kevin ogling the flowers on my desk.*

Who sent you the flowers?

A very handsome older gentleman.

Not funny Beth!

But the truth

Beth.......!

A very handsome older man, a Texan by the name of Jackson Durand.

My grandfather sent them to you?

Yes he did!

Huh!

What do you mean by "Huh"?

Just surprised

Okay I'm all ready to go.

Not in the car a good ten minutes, Kevin pulls into a parking garage off 53rd Street. Pulling in right behind us, Jerry and Dean.

Kevin why are we stopping here?

You will see

((Kevin))

Just come with me*! Taking my hand into his Kevin and I walk into Bloomindales, Tom and Jerry in tow. Knowing where this is going……*

Kevin I'm not buying anything

Fine, I am!

Great you do that but make sure every single item is solely for you. You spend your money on YOU!

Ignoring me completely Kevin leads us up several floors, ending at what seems to be a private area.

Have a seat Beth

What the hell is he up to?

Hi you must be Mr. And Mrs. Walker?

Kevin answering immediately Yes we are. Are you Sage?

I am. Mr. Walker I gathered most of what you requested. Mrs. Walker would you like to look through them?

With a very pissed look, I look Kevin in his face and respond to Sage's question Sure *and in a flash, racks of clothing are pushed in front of me. I'm going to kill this man!*

Mrs. Walker starting from the furthest end please find lounge wear, sleepwear, casual wear, business wear and right in front formal. On the table to the left shoes and handbags to match each item and on the table to the right, accessories.

Kevin handing his credit card to Sage I spurt out "What are you paying for? I haven't picked anything out yet"

Pick something out? Beth all of this is coming with us.

No...

Yes... *Handing Sage is card*

Kevin stop, you're paying for items that I may not even want... What if something doesn't fit?

Would you like to try anything on?

With a pissed look I shake my head no.

Sage returning with the receipt Thank you for all your assistance especially on such short notice. When you have everything packed, the two gentlemen over there *pointing to his left* will take them.

Mr. Walker thank you for the opportunity. Please give your grandfather my best regards.

Sage I will.

Mrs. Walker it was a pleasure to meet you. If you need anything, anything at all please do not hesitate to contact me.

With somewhat of a fake smile Thank you.

Stepping on to the escalator Kevin squeezes my hand I don't want to hear a word.

Kevin I'm furious!

Well now we are even. I was furious that you didn't purchase anything yesterday and your reason absolutely foolish!

Oh he'll no Kevin did you just say I was foolish?

No I said your reason for not shopping was foolish!

Kevin

Beth!

Trying to hold back my laughter, I burst out laughing. Anger building on Kevin's face. Kevin you're lucky I love you.

Beth, *his face softening* you really know how to get me riled up.

No you do that all on your own! But in this moment I realize this subject is not worth getting upset over.

Stopping us in place Kevin looks me directly in my eyes Mrs. Walker, if you return any item for any reason other than not fitting... we will have a problem!

Surprised, this man does know me so well. Whatever Kevin!

Okay try me

Pulling my hand away from his Oh no you don't Mrs. Walker *now kissing my hand* you can remain upset all you want. This matter is over, done with!

You just don't get it

Beth I get it... You do not want anyone taking care of you. I'm not and this needs to stop now! I am who I am.

And you met and married a very simple, low keyed woman. That is who I am.

Kissing my hand nothing simple about you. *Stopping us once again in place,* I will agree that at times having money can make a person go over the top. But Beth we are talking about necessities not cars, boats etc. So please let this be the last conversation we have on this okay?

Yes... *Portraying a fake smile*

So do you want to eat here in the City or head back to the Hamptons?

JD is leaving in the morning, I would rather have dinner with him.

Then Hampton's we go.

After almost two hours on the Long Island Expressway Kevin and I arrive at the house about eight. Entering the house I see JD sitting in the living room

Hi JD

Hello you two. How bad was the traffic?

Long Island Expressway traffic *and I laugh.*

Mrs. Clarke is keeping supper warm in the kitchen for us.

JD you haven't eaten yet?

No I was waiting for you and Kevin to arrive home.

You need to eat! *Kevin looking at me with a puzzled look* Come on let's head in. *Stopping first to use the powder room - in my world the bathroom on the first floor, Kevin and JD are already sitting.*

Assisting Mrs. Clarke I begin carrying bowls and platters of food from the stove and counter to the table. Sitting now, the three of us begin discussing JD's planned trip to Africa. Kevin and JD relive their last trip together to East Africa.

Beth you should have seen my grandson, instructing men who have spent most of their lives drilling what they needed to look for, how to go about drilling and most impressive, identifying the bedrock.

Wow Kevin, how do you know so much about drilling?

My minor was geology and *looking at his grandfather,* I had one of the best teachers.

JD eyes fill with tears. Thank you Kevin, Thank you.

Clearing the table while the two continued to talk shop, both enjoying the other's company. Would the two of you like coffee? *Barely answering me I decide to brew a pot anyway. Mrs. Clarke and Charles enters, smiling from ear to ear.*

Would you two like a cup of coffee?

No Beth, I came to clear but I see you already done so. Why don't you join the conversation, take a seat and I will serve the coffee.

Mrs. Clarke I have it.

Beth, it will be my pleasure.

Returning to my seat, conversation continued until almost eleven p.m. Looking down at my watch, I interrupt... You two gentlemen continue talking. I'm going to head up and prepare for bed.

Beth I haven't enjoyed myself like this in a very long time. Thank you!

JD I enjoyed watching the two of you discussing oil with such enthusiasm. *Walking to JD I kiss him once* that's for the beautiful flowers I received today at work, thank you and *another kiss* that's for you being so wonderful.

Turning dark red, Thank you Beth *tears developing in his eyes.*

Mr. Walker *kissing Kevin* if I'm sleep when you come up please wake me *meaning I'm in the mood.*

With a devilish smile and knowing what I am referring to, I will Beth. I'll be up in a few minutes.

Chapter Seven – Déjà vu

Good morning everyone, please take a seat. My name is Beth Walker and I'm a .... Oops wrong group *everyone laughing.* It is good to be back with you guys. But back to business, to start I want to formally introduce you to Daphne Moore. Daphne can you please tell us a little about yourself?

Present with a shy smile Hi everyone... Ah I've been here now about a week and so far my experience has been great. Um I'm from the Bronx and I'm working on my masters in social work at Hunter College. I'm looking forward to the field work and that is all I have.

Great Daphne. Beginning today you will be shadowing Pam. However if you have any questions or concerns regarding a case please feel free to come to any of us. Okay let's now talk case loads. Who would like to begin?

The department meeting finally over, I head to my office to review the agency's recent cuts. All seems to be affecting over spending - supplies, but if overhead continues to increase and state funded contracts decrease, this time next year cuts in staffing may need to happen. But for now we have to do with what we have. Deep in debate with myself I realize Paige is standing in the doorway.

Hey Paige, need something?

Stepping in and closing the door behind herself Beth you have a visitor

Paige if it is my dear and loving husband tell him…..

Interrupting, Beth not your husband but Ms. Black

The smile on my face completely disappears for me?

Yes! Beth I can tell her you're out?

Did she say what she wanted? *Trying with great difficulty to hinder my fright.*

No but when you were out she called every single day asking how you were doing.

Paige give me a few minutes then have her come in.

Beth are you sure?

With my hands shaking I'm sure Paige

Paige exits my office. Pacing back and forth I try not to think of the last time I saw Mrs. Black. Beth what happened wasn't her fault. I know this... I can do this. Trying hard not to think about that day last

summer my mind wanders to that exact day – exact time. The day my life changed forever. The day that haunts me when I least expect it to. Heavenly Father this is one of them days I ask for strength. Please help me get through this. Please do not allow me to have any resentment toward this woman and please do not allow me to dwell back on this time I so want to forget. Please father. *My prayer to my Heavenly Father is interrupted by a tap on my door*

Come in...

Mrs. Morris...

Actually, Beth Walker now.

With tears developing in her eyes, congratulations Mrs. Walker.

Thank you... Please have a seat

You look wonderful Mrs. Black. How are the kids?

Everyone is doing good and the apartment you found us is perfect. *Mrs. Black's voice cracks and tears begin to fall. Not able to hold back my own, I grab the box of tissues from my desk and walk over to where Mrs. Black is sitting. Instantly hugging her, for several seconds we sit with arms wrapped around one another*

Mrs... Beth I am so so sorry. I feel so responsible.

Barely able to speak Angela what happen was not your fault.

Beth... I'm just so sorry

I should be thanking you, my husband told me how you assisted, providing as much information as you could and for that I will be forever grateful.

I'm just so sorry...

Composing myself, so tell me about Tyrone, how is he doing in school?

Wiping tears away, he loves it Beth and as you already know, the apartment is in one if the best school districts.

What about the girls, must be so big now.

Oh they grow more everyday but wait a second. Detective Walker? You're married to Detective Walker?

Trying to suppress my smile... Yes, yes I am.

Beth no disrespect but he is FINE!

Busting out in a laugh... Ahh thanks...

Wow rising *to her feet*... Beth I'm glad you're okay and I….. Just wanted you to hear from me directly how sorry I am.

Listen today is the last day we will speak of that awful time. New beginnings for me and from what I hear for you as we'll. So we will not dwell on the past but the present and future. Deal?

Beth... Deal.

But I am glad you came by. You look great and hopefully I will be invited over to see your new place.

For you Beth an open invitation.

Thanks.... We will talk again soon. *Walking Ms. Black out, a confused look crosses her face.*

Something wrong?

Oh no I thought I saw someone that I met before.

Someone from here? Pamela and Rochelle assisted you while I was out correct?

Ah yes they did, but Beth no one could replace you. Both were great but not you.

Well I will be sure to let them both know that *giggling*

With a smile You do that and make sure you tell them I said so.

Both of us laughing, I'm glad you came by *hugging and kissing Ms. Black* I will be calling you soon to setup my visit.

I'm going to hold you to that.... See you soon.

Stepping back into the reception area I notice Donaldson standing by the elevator? He gives a half smile before I close the door.

Beth are you okay?

Paige I'm fine. The visit was actually good for me.

I'm glad.... I'm going across the street to grab some lunch, can I get you anything?

Across the street?

Oh right, yes a new deli opened. They have a great buffet bar.

Hmmm sounds good

Why don't you come with me?

Umm no I can't

Oh come on...

Clearing my head of Kevin's voice Okay let me grab my purse

Stepping out of the office an alarmed look on Mickey's or is it Donald's face.

Mrs. Walker are you going out?

Paige looking at me with somewhat of a confused look... Yes to the deli across the street.

Calling for the elevator I stand with Paige. I guess I should review who this person is but the elevator arrives. Whichever half he is of the double duo he motions for both Paige and I to stay put while he checks the elevator. With confirmation of being cleared Paige and I get in and ride down in complete silence. Walking to the deli with security in tow, I review with Paige who and why he is with us.

You're probably wondering who and why this person is with us?

Actually no Beth… I assume an undercover police officer since that woman hasn't been caught!

Yup *small white lie heavenly father!*

So Beth, did you have a chance to go through your mail?

Yes Paige I did. February 11th huh?

Yes…..

Now you're probably wondering why so soon.

No, I assumed Gregory will be shipping out soon and you want to marry before he does.

Yes and he'll be aboard the SS whatever the name for eighteen months *Paige seemingly holding back from tearing up* and it just feels right to get married now, not waiting.

When is he scheduled to report?

February 22.

Well I think it is wonderful. But will we be losing you?

No we both agree I should stay here and finish school. May is right around the corner and finally I will have my BS.

What are your plans after?

You're the first to know, other than Gregory I was accepted into NYU's School for Social Work.

Oh Paige... *hugging then kissing Paige on the cheek* Wow did you let Rochelle know?

Not yet. I just found out yesterday.

Does this mean you will be staying on, possibly taking on title of Case Worker?

With a childlike smile I was going to ask if I could.

Absolutely! Care House, me.... would be honored to have you taking on the role.

Oh Beth thank you.

And when the time comes to do the internship, don't look anywhere else. Between here and Rochelle at the Mayor's office, you are set.

Thank you so much Beth. I was a bit worried.

Paige?

I know, but with all the budget cuts.

At this time we are fine. So tell me about the wedding?

What was supposedly to be a five minute excursion out the office turned in to about a forty-five minute break? Deep in conversation neither of us notice the time. Rushing a bit now Paige and I head back. Entering the lobby of the building the other half of the double duo is in the lobby along with the lunch crowd. Walking over to building security I inquire what is going on.

Hey Harold, what's going on?

Hi Beth...... You're back *kissing me on the cheek.*

If you were working you would know these things.

Smiling I know but I needed the vacation.

So what is all this?

Oddly all four elevators are out.

All four?

Yes... Maintenance is looking into it now.

Hmmm *looking over to Batman and Robin, one is on the phone with a bleak look.*

Beth how in shape are you?

Excuse me? I have you know I am very much so in shape.... Why?

Up to a challenge? Walking up to the 17th floor?

Paige you say that as if I couldn't do it!

Well….. You're an old married lady now!

Come on, let me show you who is the fittest between the two of us… *Turing to get Abbott and Costello's attention, both are off to the side deep in conversation with someone on the phone.*

Harold when those two men are less occupied, please let them know I will meet them upstairs.

Sure Beth…. And good luck *laughing*

Very funny Mr. Brown, we will see who will be the last woman standing, let's go Mrs. 105 pounds.

Entering the stairwell I begin my incline, doing very well I must say but now reaching the 10th floor I'm losing steam.

Losing steam Beth?

Paige if I weighed no more than a hundred pounds wet I too would be bouncing around…

Ha Ha….. Hundred and five to be exact *and we both laugh.*

Stopping at the tenth floor, Paige and I rest sitting on the stairs. Suddenly a look of concern appears on each of our faces… We both first smell smoke, then see heavy clouds of smoke emerging. We both jump up and head to the door. It won't open.

What the fuck…. Paige let's try the next floor. *Running not walking, up two more flights, door locked.* This can't be happening. *Without confirming with the other, we run to the twelfth floor. Repeat of the same, door locked.*

Beth *crying* we can't get out, we are trapped!

Calm down Paige we aren't trapped. Come on we will try each door until we reach the roof.

Moving as quickly as we can, Paige and I make it to the roof and that door too is locked. The smoke becoming more intense we feel the heat of the fire.

Beth what should we do?

Stay calm…

Beth what are we going to do?

I begin banging on the door, screaming out we are hear. Considering to go back down, the smoke intensifies and the heat getting stronger. I return to banging on the door. I look over to Paige and she looks like she is having difficulty breathing.

Paige get on your knees

……

Screaming louder Paige get on your knees now! Paige listen to me.

…….

Not getting a response I go over to Paige and push her down to the ground, onto her knees. I go back to knocking on the door and just then it opens. Kevin, Erickson, Donaldson, Thomas and the Fire Department all in sight. I motion to one of the Fire Fighters to check Paige. I look up to Kevin and see a look I've never seen from him before. With no words spoken I am swooped up and carried outside. The EMS technician puts a mask over my face and begins pumping oxygen in. Still no words spoken Kevin sits me down and walks away from me. He begins talking to the Fire Chief. Erickson comes over to where I am.

How upset is he?

Beth he's pissed. Give him a few minutes to cool off.

Donaldson and Thomas? It wasn't their fault....

Beth they had instructions.....

I know. They were doing their job, I decided to take the stairs.

Beth......

Looking over to Kevin, no eye contact made. He doesn't even allow himself to look in my direction.

How is Paige?

Shaken up but ok

What the fuck did I do? Kevin and the fire chief walks over to Erickson me.

Mrs. Walker are you okay?

Yes I am. What happened?

A fire was set in the stairwell, between the 5th and 6th floor.

Set?

Yes clearly arson and all doors leading from the stairwell were locked!

I look at Kevin and his stare, looking through me rather than at me.

The fire is out and you may go back down to your office.

Looking over to Paige, she is loaded onto a stretcher. I walk over to her with tears streaming

Paige I am so sorry.

Smiling with tears falling Beth I'm okay.

Paige I will meet you at the hospital *looking at the EMS Technician* What hospital are you taking her to?

Beth Israel

Paige I will meet you and I will call your parents.

No just Gregory, the number is in my phone book.

Okay… *Paige is taken down the stairs.*

Walking back to Kevin, purposely he walks away? Feeling so alone and totally responsible I go back into the building. Hearing steps behind me I turn and Kevin is in tow. Finally on the 17th floor, I go into the office where everyone is standing around.

Beth what happened?

Pam not sure. The elevator was out so Paige and I decided to walk up the stairs. A fire began in the stairwell. Paige is being taken to Beth Israel and I'm going to meet her now. All of you go home now. The elevators are still out and due to the damage in the stairwell it would be best to take the service elevator. Pam can you gather everyone. A fireman is in the hall waiting, he will escort everyone to the service elevator then out the building.

Beth are you okay?

Forcing a smile I am. You better get going.

Grabbing Paige's purse, I take out her phone book and go into my office to call Gregory.

Hello Gregory

Yes

This is Beth Walker, I work with Paige.

Hi…. Everything okay?

We had a fire in the building. Paige is okay but she is being evaluated at Beth Israel.

I'm on my way… *The line goes dead.*

Throwing my hands to my face I hold back from falling apart. Sensing I'm not alone I remove my hands from my eyes and standing in front of me, Kevin with the same bleak look.

Everyone has left. Grab your things and we will head to the hospital.

The drive to Beth Israel - Silence. He doesn't look in my direction nor does he say a single word. Arriving I go into the emergency room and find Paige sitting up.

Hi, how are you feeling?

Beth I'm okay…..

I'm so very very sorry.

Beth it was my idea to take the stairs…

Paige…… *Just then Gregory arrives.*

Beth Gregory, Greg Beth..

Hello……

Paige what happened?

I'll explain later

Kissing Paige I'm going to give you two some privacy. Paige I will call and check in with you later.

Beth I'm okay. I Will see you tomorrow..

No, even if the doctor clears you medically, take the day. Gregory nice meeting you…..

The drive back to the Hamptons, tension so thick only an axe could cut it. Not once did Kevin look in my direction, not one word spoken. No music only "1010 wins" playing on the radio. "All news all the time". *I've never seen this side of him before. Did I go too far this time? A question I ask myself over and over again in my head.*

After a complete hour and half of silence we pull up to the front of the house. Charles waiting out on the steps. About to get out of the car Kevin motions for me to wait and I do as told. Kevin gets out and walks to the passenger side and opens the door to let me out.

Charles please meet me in grandfather's study....

I give Charles a half smile and enter the house. I go directly up to our room. Taking seat on the lounger I begin to unravel. Up to this point only tears that managed to escape presented itself but now I let go. The epiphany – my "aha" moment hits. I finally

*come to terms with the last six months of my life.
Someone is after me! And what happened today put
someone else in danger. I cry even harder at the
thought. Trying to silence my weeping cry I throw my
hands to my face. Kevin has been right all along.
What am I going to do? Crying harder I suddenly feel
sick. Jumping up and running to the bathroom I
begin vomiting over and over again. With one last
hurl I lay my head on the toilet seat. All the energy I
had is gone.*

Baby are you okay?

Back to crying Kevin I am so very sorry. You
were right..... And I put Paige in danger.

*Kevin takes a seat next to me on the floor and
wipes my face with a wet hand cloth.* Beth I can't take
this. I fucking almost lost you once before. Today,
taking the risk that you did, Beth you can't do shit
like this!

Kevin I'm sorry. I promise to follow every rule
from this point on.

Follow the rules? You do mean follow the rules
from here because no fucking way are you going
back to work.

Kevin...

Kevin me all you want. NO!

Kevin I have to go... I can't leave them like this.

Dismissing my statement Beth Mrs. Clarke has dinner waiting, let's go down.

Kevin I just need a few minutes to myself..

Beth?

Please!

Hearing the bedroom door close I pick myself up and sit on the edge of the bed. That nausea feeling resurfacing I lay across the bed waiting for it to pass.

Opening my eyes, the room is dark with a flick of a light to my right. I turn and find Kevin reading.

Feel better?

I do... What time is it?

Eleven thirty

Getting up I grab my nightgown and head to the bathroom to shower. Approximately twenty minutes later I return to the bedroom. Kevin no longer in bed? I turn the television on and begin going through the channels. Kevin returns with soup, crackers and tea.

You need to put something in your stomach.

Kevin not yet.

Then at least sip on the tea.

Thank you. Kevin please don't be upset with me.

Beth I'm not. I'm just…… Beth once again I find myself thanking God, thanking him for allowing you to see another day, not taking you from me. But Beth, this is getting tiresome.

Kevin I'm fine

Beth..

Kevin I have to go into work tomorrow. I cannot give Care House no notice. The people I work for and work with have been very accommodating. I can't do this to them.

Beth I understand.... Charles and I worked out security for tomorrow. But Beth you must give notice.

Kevin I know. The idea of putting someone, putting Paige in danger, I would never forgive myself.

Taking me into his arms, Beth…….

Kevin I know...

Kissing me, Baby I have a short list of people in my life to protect, to lay my life down for and you're at the top of the list. It is killing me that I can't keep you safe.

Kevin..... I now know what my lack of thinking and poor decisions do. I finally get it now and until this person is caught, I will do what is expected of me. I love you Mr. Walker and I am truly sorry.

I love you....

Chapter Eight – Reputation Saves The Day?

Friday finally here I can't say my first week back hasn't been uneventful because it certainly has. Another hour and this endless week will be over.

Knock... Knock....

Come in

Beth walker?

Immediately to my feet Yes, Mr. Goldfarb how are you? How can I help you?

Beth please have a seat. I received a call from Jackson Durand.

Holy shit, JD what did you do?

Small world, JD and I served together many many years go in the army.

Oh? *Fuck am I losing my job? I already put my notice in. Why is the CEO and President of Bell International Electronics here, in my office? Care house is a drop in the bucket for him. His wife's pet project from what I've been told? Shit...*

JD told me you're his grand-daughter in law?

Ah... Yes

Don't worry I understand the need to keep this quiet.

Thank you

So, my reason for personally meeting with you. Starting Monday you will be working from a home office. You will maintain your title and position until Kevin and JD confirms no further threats exists.

Mr. Goldfarb, sir that won't be necessary. I already gave notice.

And as of this moment not accepted. To be very honest young lady before talking to JD I had no idea who you were or what goes on here. But since, I talked to a few people about you and young lady you seem to be well respected around here.

Thank you

No need to explain to anyone, all is done and in motion.

Mr. Goldfarb, thank you.

No young lady, from what my wife and I learned you have gone above and beyond your duties. We thank you. When you talk to JD let him know I expect to see him at the Hampton Classic this Memorial Day.

I will Mr. Goldfarb and again thank you.

As quickly as he came is as quickly he leaves. How is Kevin going to feel about this? Continuing to work here? But at least it will be from home for the most part? Oh JD saving the day but Kevin, this isn't going to go well.

Knock…. Knock…

Come in

Beth, was that really Joshua Goldfarb? Owner of Bell International Electronics?

Yes it was

Reason for the visit?

Think quick Beth…. Come on! Umm, he heard what has been going on here and wanted to insure we were doing okay.

Really?

Hmm seems so. Also to let me know if I wanted to remain on board I could.

Wow Beth, I hope you said yes?

I did. But until this person is caught I will be working from home starting Monday. I will however come into the office as needed.

Great, because I don't think I would stay on if you weren't here.

Oh Paige, you don't make a decision like that based on one person! But thank you.

Beth you will sill attend my wedding?

Paige, I……

Oh Beth you have to come!

Paige…..

No, if I have to make room for your security I will do that.

Paige Kevin and I will be in attendance. We look forward to it.

Great. Beth do you need me for anything else?

No you head home and I will talk to you on Monday. Enjoy your weekend.

Thanks Beth, you too. Oh and yes the two gentleman are waiting patiently in the waiting area.

Alright, I'm packing up now. Good night Paige. *As Paige leaves my office Kevin enters.* Mr. Walker I had a feeling you would be picking me up. *Kissing Kevin.*

Yes baby…. Ready to go?

I am…. *Turning lights off and checking to insure all doors are locked, Kevin, Donaldson, and I leave. Walking out the building I see Charles standing outside of that sweet ride he picked us up from the airport in.*

Kevin where's your car?

I requested Thomas drive it home so you and I could have a relaxing ride home.

Alright Kevin, what are you up to?

Not a thing. Come on let's head home.

Sitting comfortably we begin the long journey to the Hamptons.

So, Mrs. Walker how was your day?

Shit he knows something Quiet. Paige wanted to insure we would be attending her wedding.

What did you tell her?

Initially hesitant but told her we would be attending.

Great... Anything else?

Well *here I go* Joshua Goldfarb came to see me today.

Joshua Goldfarb of Bell International Electronics?

Yes

And what did he want?

Do not get mad! Promise me!

Go ahead Beth...

JD seems to know him.... And

Laughing Beth I know all about it. Joshua and my grandfather are old friends.

You know him too?

Yes but it was only through a thorough security check Charles conducted that we found the connection between Goldfarb and Care House.

So he basically rejected my letter of resignation based on his relationship with you and JD? *The look of disappointment must be written all over my face.*

Actually no. After making a few calls he called my grandfather back and told him how much you are valued at Care House.

Right!

No really, JD only reviewed the need to work from home during this time. It was solely you and your work ethic that got him to agree.

Blushing.... So you're on board with this.

Absolutely baby…..

I have to say I was worried I would have a fight on my hands…

I know how important this job is to you.

Are you concerned about Mr. Goldfarb knowing about us?

No, Goldfarb is one of my grandfather's oldest and most trusted friends… No concerns.

Realizing we just went over the George Washington Bridge Kevin where in the hell are we going?

Flashing that devilish smile... You trust me?

Of course I do.

Then just enjoy the ride. You and I are both off tomorrow so no rush.

Kevin!

Relax! Charles could you please push that CD in?

Just then the sound of Natalie Cole fills the cabin and I take off my coat and shoes and semi lay against Kevin.

Don't fall asleep on me, we are almost there.

Where?

Look out the window

Charles pulls off a main road and stops at a privacy gate to enter a code.

Kevin where are we?

Keep looking.......

Once through the gate and about a mile into the driveway we stop in front of a massive colonial home.

What a stunning home. Who lives here?

Only one way to find out.

I Put my shoes and coat back on and step out of the vehicle with Charles's assistance. Kevin already at my side.

Here you go baby *handing me a set of keys*

Kevin you didn't?

I did and before you get pissed please just take a look.

Opening the front door, I step into a magnificent foyer that screams "welcome home". Stepping further in, a large great room with a dual staircase

Kevin?

Baby keep looking...

What's the square footage?

6,500 on 3 acres of land

Kevin!

Baby, if you don't like it we will stay in the Hamptons until we find something.

Did you buy this?

I did but I got it at a bargain and will put it back on the market if you want me to. *Taking my hand* Let me show you something.

Walking with Kevin through the house we end in the back yard. Baby, you have the Hudson River at your door.

My God Kevin…

Like a child on Christmas Kevin guides me back into the house, to a room off the formal living room Open the door

What?

Open the door

Opening the door I turn on the light to find a fully furnished office Kevin … *Hugging him.* For me?

All yours and everything you need to get your workday going on Monday!

Wait, we aren't going back to the Hamptons?

Not if you don't want to….

But…

But what? The two most important rooms have been furnished, your office and the bedroom which we should go up and see…

Excited I in turn, grab Kevin's hand and drag him upstairs. Opening all doors, so far I've seen five empty rooms and two hall bathrooms. Opening the last door completely at the end of the hallway I'm in complete awe. The bedroom is spectacular. Kevin this is absolutely beautiful.

Check out the bathroom

Scanning the room for the right door to enter, I open a door to a dressing area. A dressing room?

Yes your walk-in closet / Dressing area!

Kevin all the clothing and shoes I own would get swallowed up in here.

You could remedy that instantly. Better yet I could because I know you will not *flashing a disapproval look*. But for now open that door.

Following Kevin's instructions I open a door that leads to a bathroom the size of my apartment. Holy crap!

Beth do you like it?

Kevin I love it! *My eyes begin to swell. I sit on the bed and take in the scenery. Kevin sits by my side and begins undressing me.*

Kevin what are you doing?

I'm going to make love to my wife, in our new home, in our new bed!

What about Thomas, Donaldson and Charles?

Don't worry about them, Charles is working on the security parameters and Thomas and Donaldson are assisting.

Kevin…..

No excuses woman, we have all that we need. Food in the fridge downstairs for nourishment and in that overnight bag clothes for the next few days. Did I miss anything?

Baby not a thing. *In this moment I kiss my husband passionately. I begin assisting Kevin with unbuttoning my blouse. I stand to step out of my skirt. I sit back on the bed and I undo Kevin's belt, unzip his pants and motion for him to step out of them. I stand now unbuttoning Kevin's shirt and pulling it off. The last items on each of us are our underwear. About to pull Kevin's off, my hand is grabbed and I am picked up and gently placed onto the bed. I lay back to allow for my panties to be taken off. But I am taken by surprise, my panties are pulled half way down my legs and in an instant I feel Kevin's mouth on me. I attempt to push his head away but instantly my arms are grabbed and I am pinned. A battle between my head and lower extremities, my lower half takes lead. My protest declines and vocal expressions of my enjoyment fills the room. Unable to retain my need to release* Kevin please stop.

Stop? ….. Why?

Because I want you in me.

Oh I will be but I want you to enjoy this and the only way I will know is by you releasing. So let go and enjoy!

Kevin no.… *And in this moment I do as I'm told. Pressure building within me to the point of almost being painful I begin to let go.*

Baby do you know how much I love you?

I do Kevin - I do *and in this moment and out of my control I find my lower half grinding against Kevin's mouth. Then it happens a whaling cry comes from me*

Baby that's what I was waiting for. *Kevin instantly removes my panties as well as his underwear. He is now inside me and all I want from him this very moment is for him to thrust into me forcefully. To go as deep as he can. Instantly my want is met. Feeling completely free with my man, I motion for him to get off of me. As if he already knows my motive, with no words Kevin stands behind me and I bend over to invite him in once more. Instantly reacting to this overwhelming pleasure my release comes instantly, confirming my appeasement ((*Oh Kevin))*. Grasping my breast forcibly but yet pleasurably Kevin pulls me into him, repeating over and over again. Then with one last ever so pleasing* *thrust and hearing his voice* My love *it happens. With his words I feel that now familiar fill. In response once again I release but this time the sensation last longer and with Kevin now caressing my back and neck with his tongue I release once again. Differently from all other times I find myself completely exhausted. Laying completely on top of my husband I find myself panting like a puppy after a long day of play.*

Beth, thank you!

Barely able to speak For what?

My happiness!

Oh Kevin, I should be thanking you.

Baby can I ask you a question?

Sure

About sex? I know you're a bit shy about the subject.

With a hesitant look Ask your question Mr. Walker and depending on the question I may or may not answer.

Beth I know I'm not your first but there seems to be some unawareness? Maybe I'm using the wrong word to describe…

Let me guess you notice something different back on the island, our first morning?

And each time since!

Kevin, when I tell you I never enjoyed sex, not an exaggeration. It was a chore, nothing pleasurable about it. The first time with you I don't know, I felt love but I wasn't ready to allow myself to enjoy the moment, to be completely free with you.

What changed then?

I don't know. Our first time on the island I stop thinking and allowed my heart to guide me, to trust you completely. And I am glad I did because I have never experienced what I have with you.

Oh baby…. The pressure is on….

Kevin, I realized it isn't anything that can be forced, it just happens. My loving you is all that is needed.

Hope you say that fifty years from now.

You plan to keep jumping my bones in our eighties? *Smiling*

Absolutely. I may need to be propped, tucked and held to maintain balance but hell yes. You and I will be lovers to the end

Laughing You say that now Mr. Walker but when I am sagging and dragging I'm going to remind you of this moment.

I'm going to hold you to that. So Beth, am I forgiven?

Forgiven for what?

Purchasing the house!

Yes you are. But what's the mortgage payments?

Beth?

Monthly note? Payment?

Okay don't get upset, no note. It is paid for!

((Kevin))

Beth we needed a home. Come on baby I can give you plenty of other reasons to get pissed.

With a smile emerging upon my face Yes you could. I love the house, thank you *kissing him on the lips. Climbing off of Kevin I stand and begin looking for something to put on.*

Would I happen to have a robe here?

You do Mrs. Walker but where are you going?

Exploring, seeing how much it is going to cost to furnish this place and YOU Mr. Walker will not be contributing one single cent!

Beth!

That's my name. Now a robe please!

Five in the morning on a Saturday. I laid here as long as I can. I can't wait to tour this house once more. Magnificent is the only word that comes to mind to describe it. Everything I expressed I wanted in my home, my wish list. And in this moment I remember the day after Thanksgiving, Kevin and I laying on the floor taking in the beautiful Christmas tree he and I just decorated. Kevin asked me to describe the perfect home. Based on what I saw so far he listened to each and every detail. I look over at my husband. Even in his sleep he is the finest man I ever met. Getting out of bed I am grabbed by the waist.

Baby where are you going?

Kevin I tried to sleep but I'm just too excited. I have a need to go exploring again.

Beth what time is it?

Almost six.

Releasing me and getting up himself Okay let's go exploring.

No you go back to sleep

Nope already up. But Beth I didn't get a chance to discuss something with you last night.

Discuss what Kevin?

Mrs. Clarke, I would like to ask her to stay on and work for us.

Kevin?

Beth, she no longer works for my grandfather and she hasn't for many years.

Then why is she here?

My grandfather asked her to come. Mrs. Clarke has always been the mediator between my grandfather and me. Beth near the boat dock is a small cottage, Mrs. Clarke could stay there.

What about her family?

Mrs. Clarke is a widow and no children.

Baby, sure.

Beth, this means a lot to me. Thank you.

Your welcome Mr. Walker. Now I have a request for you.

I don't think I like where this is going

Hear me out. My car, my baby, time to get her back.

Beth…..

Come on, we are several bridges away from the city and just to go locally. I will even agree to security following me.

…………..

I need my car man…. My fix…… I'm going through withdrawal….. *Kevin and I begin to laugh*

Beth I swear, your detail better be wherever you are!

Climbing on top of Kevin I give you my word.

Alright, we can go car shopping.

How in the hell do you get car shopping out of I need MY car? Kevin I don't need to go car shopping, I have a car and a note I am comfortable with…..

Beth your car is known. I'm positive whoever is behind this knows your car. Time to let go!

Anger building and expressed through my voice No! I have a car. All I would like is to be taken to the Hamptons to pick it up or someone driving it up here.

That's all you want!

Stop playing Kevin, which is it?

You getting a new car with new plates! When you agree to that then we can talk *motioning me to get off him*

Two can play this game Oh baby, I don't mean to get you upset. *Kissing Kevin on the mouth then licking and kissing his neck.*

Beth!

Baby I don't want to fight, *moving my mouth down Kevin's front* over something so silly *licking the lower half of his stomach and. stopping short at his man hood. Looking up at Kevin, eyes closed and manhood at attention* but when I get my car back in my possession I will be more than happy to finish what you are expecting right this moment. *I hop off of Kevin and laugh hard.*

Oh that is cold! Beth just wrong

Wrong but right. Whatever you feel it is, I love you.

And I love you *Kevin kisses me hard. This fucking man, I have to have him now. I guess no car!*

Chapter Nine – Moving On Up

How in the hell are we going to furnish this big ass house? Here less than twenty four hours and I've gotten lost twice. I need to draw a diagram and label each and every room.

Ding Dong ……… Ding Dong….

What the hell?

Yelling from the kitchen Beth can you get the door?

I guess I can. I'm just as close as you are! I can get the door with no problem but my car is left all the way in the Hamptons and you had nerve to make love to me knowing I was attempting an ultimatum…. *Ha Ha… But it was good as* Who is it?

Beth is that the way one answers the door when they move on up?

((Cynthia)) *fighting to unlock the door. Once open I'm eye to eye with my beautiful sister, hugging her tight* Oh my God I've missed you.

I missed you too *kissing me* but this psychotic cat misses you more.

Tiger… Cynthia come, come in

Look at you all tanned.

Cynthia I missed you but who, how did you get here?

Your husband sent Mark to pick me up.

Mark? Who in the hell is Mark?

Mark Donaldson? Doesn't he work for Kevin?

Had no idea he was a Mark. Works for Kevin's grandfather.

Where's my handsome brother in law?

Did I hear someone mention me? *Kevin bear hugs Cynthia.* Was the drive okay?

For me yes, for Mark... You know I was a backseat driver. *We all laugh...*

Beth I'm going to give you and Cynthia some time alone. I need to go into the city for a bit.

But you're off...

Yes but sometimes duty calls even when I'm off. You and Cynthia catch up. I'll be back as soon as I can. Anyone rings the gate let Charles take care of it. He has a team coming in to upgrade the security system. Only Charles should interact with anyone requesting entrance..... Okay!

Yes baby. Don't worry I'll be too occupied talking about you.

Glad I'm leaving then *Kissing Cynthia* If I hadn't met your sister first

Blushing, Mr. Walker I'm too much woman for you, literally! *We laugh*

Sweetheart, enjoy your sister and I will be back as soon as I can. *Switching from his joking personality to "your my only concern"* Remember you promised to follow all the rules Beth. Please if your inner voice suggest you do something that you know I will be against please talk it out with Cynthia…. Please!!!!

I'm not two….. I will. I love you.

Alright ladies see you later…..

Soo Mama, tour first then that large pot of tea?

Lead the way…………

After giving Cynthia a complete tour of the house and the immediate backyard, my sister and I finally sit and talk over the long awaited pot of tea. Stretched across my bed I begin to update my sister on all that has happen.

So Mr. Walker is the grandson of Jackson Durand…..

Yup… But Cynthia do you know who Jackson Durand is? What his company does or owns?

Beth please tell me you know who this man is? One of the biggest manufacturers of oil?

No…. *embarrassed* but I am learning?

Beth….

What?

The man is forever in the news. And now that I think about it, years ago it came out he had a biracial grandson, shortly after his son was killed. Wow! It was hushed up immediately but it did come out!

Well I can say he is a very sweet man. Kevin says he tries to get him to work with him.

What about his grandmother?

My heartbreaks for Kevin, she rejected him a long time ago. JD has been the only influence from his father's side.

Wow…..

Let's not mention finding out my husband is bi-racial…..

Laughing… What about it Beth…. Need I remind you Kevin's skin color is darker than you my baby Casp

You better not!

What, I was only asking if you saw the latest episode of Casper The Friendly Ghost?

Cynthia! *We both laugh...*

Ring ….. Ring…….

Where's my cell?

Ring …. Ring…..

Here it is… Hello?

Beth?

Yes….. Who is this?

You can't go far. I will find you very very soon and strike when you least expect!

Who the fuck is this….. Hello??

Don't worry about who I am, be worried of what I am capable of. Be worried that I will not fail this time.

Hello? *The line goes dead*

Beth who was that

Shaking uncontrollably, No one…..

Beth… Who was it?

I don't know….

What did they say?

I can't go far, I will find you very very soon and strike when you least expect *Inhaling deeply* and this time I won't fail.

((CALL KEVIN NOW)))

No *scrambling for my keys*

BETH!

Cynthia don't worry I got this.

Got it how? This is the shit Kevin talks about!

Running down the stairs to the front door Beth where in the hell are you going?

To find Charles and Donaldson.

Beth wait, let me do it.

Cynthia I got it…

No, sit your ass down. Where's my pocketbook? Beth this isn't a joke. My God why is this happening? *Pulling out her cell phone*

Cynthia who are you calling?

Beth just….. Shit his voice mail? Kevin call the house as soon as you can. Everyone is fine. Just call. *Hanging up* Lock the door behind me.

If I'm not going out, you're not going out!

Beth no time for fucking jokes, sit your ass down and lock the door.

Sit down and lock the fucking door? *We both laugh* Cynthia let's calm down. Its dark out and we / I have no idea where Charles and Donaldson are at *I begin laughing uncontrollably.* We are in the woods in fucking Rockland County *laughing so hard tears are trickling down my face* and we are sitting her like a fucking horror movie…

Beth stop, this shit isn't funny *Cynthia now crying but laughing*…. I have to pee…..

Walking together, we go into the bathroom off the living room….

Go ahead I will wait here.

Oh no you won't, get your ass in here.

Both of us in the bathroom Cynthia pee! Hurry up! Do you think we should call the police? Fuck *laughing harder* I don't know the address…. I don't know the address to my own home……

Moving nervously around, accidently I turn off the light. Panicking Cynthia and I bust out of the bathroom, falling onto the floor. Cynthia barely with her panties up, we are confronted not only by Kevin but Charles and Donaldson.

Beth, what the fuck are you doing?

Both Cynthia and I laughing so hard tears of fright trickling down our faces.

Someone called me on my cell phone and *laughing harder* said….

Ahem…. Ah could you gentleman turn your heads but help me up?

What the fuck is going on?

Helping Cynthia up, Kevin has a look pure anger Beth!

Someone called my cell and said "You can't go far, I will find you very very soon and strike when you least expect"

Beth the rest

Cynthia

Beth what the fuck was said?

Kevin just letting me know whomever it is will not fail this time.

With a pissed alarmed look And your standing here fucking laughing....

Trying to stop laughing but the giggles continue, Ahem no Kevin we - we were trying to figure out what to do and ….. Ahem…. Cynthia had to pee! And *the uncontrollable laughter resumes……*

Beth give me the GOD DAMN PHONE!

Handing Kevin the phone Cynthia let's leave these fine me to their work *and the laughter continues*

Beth are you drunk? Are you high?

Nope…

Beth, this shit isn't funny

And in this moment my laugher turns into pure anger with anger tears. Don't you think I fucking know that? Don't you? I can't leave my fucking house? I can't drive? I can't live my life because some PYCHOTIC FUCK is after me and I have no idea, no clue as to why! Tonight I fucking did not know what to do. And the only parent I have is her and what did I do? I now put her in danger. So yes I know how serious this is! Don't – do not fucking come down on me like this…. I know too well and reality tonight, I have to now worry about you and Cynthia.

Beth…

Kevin……. Just let me be! *Walking toward the stairs* Cynthia zip your damn pants up *and I make my way to my bedroom.*

Approximately fifteen minutes later Kevin enters our bedroom.

Are you okay?

Yes Kevin

Look at me!

Kevin I'm not in the mood to do this.

Well too bad. Do you think I purchased this house to run from the problem? Well I did. I will spend every fucking dime I have and lay my life on the line to keep you safe. I'm sorry this is happening. I wish to God I knew why. But I don't. I understand this is hard for you. Baby I know this. But I can't have you losing it. My fault if I didn't put a better plan in place. But I assure you and promise as of tonight every precaution will be in place to keep you safe in your home.

Kevin you're missing the point. Life behind the gate? That's it for me?

For now it is….. And if and when you go out having security with you. You told me after the fire you understood… I'm taking you at your word.

Kevin what do you want me to say?

Tell me you will not give up. Tell me you will adhere to the demands I may set upon you to insure your safety. Tell me you will take the necessary precautions to protect yourself. *Taking my hand…* Promise me!

I promise!

Kissing me on the cheek, Come with me

Where?

Just come on….. *Following Kevin we go downstairs and enter the garage….* Before you go into another fit of rage, you still have your car and your car note. But *handing me the keys* you are now the owner of your own 550i Beamer.

Kevin!

Look if you're about to…..

I love it… *Kissing Kevin* Thank you.

Great…. But after tonight Beth security will be tighter, understand?

I do

Okay where's Cynthia ((Cynthia))) Cynt…

Stepping into the garage cautiously Is it safe?

Well your sister hasn't taken me out yet, I'm still standing.

With somewhat of a pissy look Funny Kevin!

Wasn't trying to be! But I think we should get out. Beth up to driving us a bit in your new car?

I think I can manage that. *Delaying my entrance into the car until Cynthia is settled in I motion to Kevin to join me at the back of the car.*

Kevin I apologize for the tone, forgive me?

Baby I understand. I look forward to the day we can look back on this day and appreciate the humor of it. But baby, even seeing your sister in such a vulnerable position, all that registers is the "what if's".

But you have to admit, Cynthia and I falling out of the bathroom had to be hilarious… *laughing*

Actually, it scared the shit out of us. I don't think you notice but Beth our weapons were drawn. I did not know what to expect after getting Cynthia's message and getting your voice mail when calling you and Cynthia back. That's why I was so upset. Do you know what could have happened?

I do now….

Good cause I could use a drink and a meal.

Ah should I ask about my phone?

Charles is handling it. Will know something when we get back. Now feed me woman!

Eek. I'm really milking you tonight. No cash could you flick a few bucks my way?

I got you baby!

Chapter Ten – And The Honoree Is?

Baby feeling any better?

A bit. What are you doing home?

I took the day off

Trying to suppress my nausea feeling I force a smile You took the day off? *Mrs. Clarke even seems surprise.*

Beth what would you like for breakfast?

Nothing Mrs. Clarke

Beth you haven't eaten in three days. *Mrs. Clark's voice expressing concern.*

Beth maybe you should go to the doctor.

Kevin it isn't anything. Between not being able to shake this flu, being anemic and preparing for tonight I'm just a little run down. *From the corner of my eye I notice the eye exchange between Mrs. Clarke and Kevin.* Something you two want to share?

Beth we are just concerned.

Listen you two, I'm fine *however get me to the nearest toilet because whatever little food is in me is about to come up. I jump from my seat and rush to the bathroom off the kitchen. I immediately begin gagging but nothing comes up. I can only manage foam and just in this moment it hit me, I've been here before.* Oh my fucking God, no this can't be. Please.

What's wrong Beth?? *An alarmed look on Kevin's face.*

I begin to cry. The more I think about what this probably is I cry harder.

Beth you're scaring me, what the fuck is wrong?

Composing myself I stand, rinse my mouth and wash my face. Kevin looking at me, waiting for an answer.

Beth???

Kevin it isn't anything, no worries. I'm going to lay down for a little bit. I'm fine.

Your fine with tears streaming down your face?

Attempting to force a smile I'm fine...... *I make my way back upstairs. The nausea feeling returning I go into the bathroom and sit on the edge of the tub.* Stupid, stupid.... This can't be.... No God please no I don't want this. I can't do this. Please no.... *I begin weeping once more. Without a knock or forewarning Kevin enters the bathroom and sits beside me.*

Sighing Could it be your pregnant?

Kevin's question completely unravels me. My crying now loud and hard. Kevin takes me into his arms and begins to rock me. No words spoken and no need to repeat the question. My noted emotions answers.

Kevin I think I am. Please don't hate me for my reaction, my not wanting children hasn't changed. *Weeping* Please don't hate me…. Please!

Beth *Lifting my head to look at him* I told you I would be fine either way. I love you Beth and I certainly would never force you to do something you didn't want to.

Kevin….. I'm so sorry….

Get some rest, you have a big evening ahead of you tonight. *Changing the subject* Are you prepared?

I think I am.

Kevin now talking to me from his dressing area Beth what are you wearing?

One of the gowns you purchased on our honeymoon.

Hmmm, well Cynthia and I met for lunch last week and we found this old rag……

What did you do?

Try it on…

Kevin the spending!

Oh try it on………

161

Putting the long black gown on I immediately fall in love. Turning to Kevin Do you like?

No I don't like, I love. Baby you look stunning.

I love the gown, thank you.

Alright, are you okay up here? I'm going to water the rose bushes I planted last week.

I still can't believe my husband a gardener, who knew!

Funny Beth…. And if Erickson calls can you have Mrs. Clarke get me immediately?

Everything alright?

Yes Beth no worries.

After sleeping the morning and part of the afternoon away I am awaken by my sister hovering over me

Hey sleeping Beauty time to get up.

Hey Cynthia, when did you get here?

About ten minutes ago. I was told you haven't been feeling well?

Sighing Cynthia….. *Tears begin to fall*

Stop it…. Tonight is a big night for you. Whatever it is we can face it tomorrow.

Where's Kevin?

In the back planting pine trees along the back fence?

Cynthia and I both laugh... Yes my husband the gardener. He refuses to hire a landscaper. The one area I will not argue with him on.

Beth who does he remind you of?

I know, daddy.... Cynthia I swear if I hear the words "You're stepping on my grass"

Ha ha.... You married your father

Really!

Cynthia could you make us a cup of tea and I will jump into the shower?

Sure

About to step into the shower a knock at the bathroom door.

Come in!

Entering, Kevin. Hey I thought you were Cynthia

She and Mrs. Clarke are discussing smothered pork chops I think.

Stepping in, closing and locking the door. Kevin what's wrong?

I have this *In hand a pregnancy test*

Kevin?

If you want to have a better idea in terms of what is actual, we can find out now.

If I am, my feelings are not going to change

I know Beth....

Alright *opening the box* Are you going to stay?

Can I?

Kevin? Do you think I wouldn't tell you the truth?

Beth poor decision making an issue not honesty.

At least turn your head.....

Beth????

An awkward smile emerges... Fine! I sit on the toilet and literally pee on a stick. Resting the test on tissue I notice the two lines developing instantly while washing my hands. My smile now gone and replaced with tears. Kevin informed of the positive status by way of my tears.

Kevin I'm sorry..... *In this moment Kevin grabs me tightly and hugs me.*

I will support any decision you make Beth. Honey I love you and that will never ever change.

Composing myself, a knock at the door.

Beth everything okay?

Ah sorry Cynthia.... I will be out in a second.

Discarding the box and test I put my robe on. About to open the door, Kevin takes me into his arms and kisses me passionately. Opening the door he calls for Cynthia who is in another room. When she arrives…. My beautiful wife is all yours, for the moment! *Kevin flashes that ever so handsome smile and leaves the room.*

Everything okay Beth?

Yes it is…..

Okay we are running behind. Take your shower and I'm going to dress.

By 5:15 Cynthia and I are completely dressed. Cynthia you look beautiful.

So do you!

Thank You.

Before we head down I just want you to know how proud I am of you.

Cynthia don't make me cry…. Please!

Just know your success - your achievements are a testament of only you. No one could ever take that credit.

No one other than you! Year to date without you in my life guiding me, who knows what my life would be like.

Tears streaming down my sister's face Come on let's head down

Holding back my tears Where's Kevin?

He asked that you meet him in the library. The library. Wow! Baby girl you have come a long way.

Making our way downstairs I enter the library as requested. Kevin turns the NCAA game off when he sees me.

Baby each and every time you stun me with your beauty.

Hey Mr. Walker, what are you doing in here all alone?

I wanted a few minutes with my wife, to give her this *in hand a black velvet box.* Open it.

Kevin I'm going to kill you. *Inside beautiful pearls* The pearls are exquisite, black pearls thank you.

Yes baby *and as Kevin places the strand around my neck, I'm being kissed very sensually...*

Mr. Walker my sister is waiting for us!

Okay... okay but Elizabeth tonight you being honored, I am very proud of you. I've told you many times before how magnificent you are. This award tonight confirms I'm not the only person who feels this way.

Baby I love you, thank you.

Okay let's head out. *Walking to the front door Cynthia request that I come into the living room.*

Cynthia what's wrong? *As I enter, to my surprise the most important people in my life are standing and applauding. I instantly begin to cry.*

Everyone please lift your glass and help me toast tonight's honoree, my wife Elizabeth Lillian Cook - Walker!

Here here...... Congratulations.

To my surprise, JD, Adele and John, Rochelle and of course my sister all here, for me and with me. I turn to Kevin and whisper "I love you"!

Okay the limo awaits. Let's get going.

Driving into Manhattan, conversation in the limousine range from today's politics to the NCAA Playoffs. Kevin holding my hand and often kissing it as we ride. JD on the other side of me whispers "You're bound for greatness young lady. This proves it". *I kiss JD and begin staring out of the window. I begin thinking about my dad not being here, not being a part of this, to be here in this limo with the*

*people who mean the most to me. Then my thoughts
hovers around what I have to face tomorrow and how
my decision is going to affect Kevin. Tears forming in
my eyes Kevin squeezes my hand. His show of
affection heavies my heart even more and the tears
fall faster. All conversation in the limousine stops
and I feel all eyes on me.*

JD could I switch seats with you?

Sure darling, *referring to Cynthia.*

*By my side Cynthia takes my other hand and
whispers in my ear* Beth are the tears for daddy or the
pregnancy?

I immediately smile Cynthia how do you know?

Because Beth you haven't been yourself and the
flu has lingered too long. As to daddy….. I miss him
too and not having him here to celebrate is difficult.
But you know in your heart he is here.

I know……

*To allow Cynthia and I some sort of privacy,
Kevin leads the chatter with the status of the NCAA
conference and the next big thing coming out of St.
John's. Although a good effort only he, JD and John
interacts.*

For the remainder of the drive into the city I sit with Kevin to my right holding and squeezing my hand. Looking at me often and winking each time. He whispers in my ear how much he loves me and publicly refers to me as "my love" when mentioning me in his conversation with our family. On the left of me my sole support for many years. Her looking at me reminds me of my childhood. Always by my side to help me onto my feet when I fell and even to this day when I fall. In this moment I realize the many blessings God has bestowed upon me.

Ladies and gentleman, I would like to begin the evening by welcoming you all. My husband and I have supported Care House now for 35 five years, this year makes our 35th year. *Applause* And for the past 25 years we have held this same dinner – fundraiser but this is the first time we exceeded all expectations. Look around you, a completely packed – full house, not one empty seat. *Applause* And another first, up to this year our honorees have been more so our benefactors, our financial supporters. Differently this year, we looked in house. We looked at the people who conducts the day to day business, who are in the trenches. Although this agency is filled with dedicated workers, one particular person stood out, Mrs. Elizabeth Walker. *Applause*

Beth, you have no idea how many phone calls and letters I received from families you have worked with. Many no longer receiving services through Care House but yet you continue to call just to see how things are going. One woman called me to say you should've been honored years ago *the crowd laughs.* You not only helped her with her domestic situation but insure year after year her children are enrolled in camp during the summer, activities during school breaks and more importantly has food on the table and gifts under the tree for the holidays ."Beth would come by days before each holiday to make sure we have food and gifts. She would say, great to have food on the actual holiday but you and the kids have to eat on those other days". When this woman told Beth "I could never repay you for what you do", Beth's response was "to repay me simply do for another. Assist an older person by carrying a package, let them in front of you in the grocery store. Volunteer when you can and drop a can of food into a donation box if able". *Turning to me* Beth absolutely beautiful. Another example of your generosity and compassion, I received a letter from a young woman regarding her sister and niece.

The smile that was upon my face just went away. Please don't do this, don't go any further. Kevin immediately takes my hand into his. I begin to shake.

This woman wanted me to know that Beth was more than a Case Worker but a super hero to her sister. "Whenever my sister or niece needed anything at all Beth was the first to assist".

Tears begin to fall down my face…

And based on the many phone calls and letters I received "Super Hero" would be the appropriate title. With no further ado, our honoree and recipient of Care House Person of the Year, I give you Mrs. Elizabeth Walker.

Kevin stands and extends his hand to help me up. Once standing he escorts me to the podium and kisses me gently. Walking back to his seat I'm here to face this crowd alone.

Thank you Mrs. Goldfarb. I too was surprise to hear that I'm the first to receive this award as an employee of Care House. All that you just heard about me didn't come all that naturally. In fact when I came to Care House I was a young naive girl who needed a lot *smiling* I mean a lot of guidance and luckily for me my mentor who was and is to this day ever so patient, kind and understanding held my hand when needed and released it when she felt I no longer needed the support. *Pointing to Rochelle* Rochelle Horowitz thank you for everything. Without you the compassion, understanding with a mix of not backing downess would not be. *With a smile and nod Rochelle acknowledges and the crowd applaud her as I do.*

I guarantee no one other than the more experienced Case Workers here tonight can pick out an abused victim in this room. Domestic violence does not discriminate, it's an equal opportunist. It happens in every culture, every religion, and every walk of life. From the wealthiest to the poorest, it occurs. In this room we exists. Yes I say we because I was one of the statistics, a number. *I look over to Kevin who shines that supportive smile. With a nod from him I continue.* For several years I was married to a man that literally expressed his love with an open hand… Baby I love you "smack" but why do you make me do this. Yes that was my life. Black eyes, hand prints around my neck, face, arms, legs, broken bones that weren't immediately attended to. That was my life.

Now the kicker, many of you are internally asking why I didn't just go – leave. I stand here to testify how difficult that feat is. Oh I had plenty of chances to leave. But shame and pride were my hindrance. Worrying about what the neighbour was going to say, how my family would react. Worrying what church members would do. Not that easy. Then when you do muster the courage you wonder how I'm going to support myself, where will I live. How will I live? Just when you think you took two big steps forward by overcoming shame and pride you're knocked back two feet by how will I live!

For me, my start over didn't come so easily. I didn't get over shame nor pride and had no answers to the how. Instead, after my final brutal attack I attempted to take my life. *Smiling* Luckily for me God rejected me and gratefully he did because I am able to experience real love. And let me tell ya *bigger smile* nothing better in the world. *Laughing and applause from the crowd. Looking at Kevin who has somewhat of an embarrassed look on his face* Sorry to out you baby....

I know I'm rattling on, this wasn't the speech I prepared and worked on for the past two weeks but it feels right to share my own personal story, to put a known face with Domestic Violence. Domestic Violence has no boundaries and it occurs across all economical classes. So tonight I accept this award for my sisters who didn't make it to see light again. I accept this award for my sisters who are. I accept this award for my sisters who will unfortunately be. I accept this award on behalf of my co-workers *pointing to the table in the center where Paige, Rochelle, Pam, Daphne and Robert are seated.* I accept and thank my sister *looking at Cynthia* I love you and my wonderful husband who has shown me what love and partnership really is. I accept this award and thank you all.

Looking out across the room, everyone is on their feet. A standing ovation. I look over to Cynthia who is wiping tears away, Adele and John who didn't know my story knows now and they both are wiping their eyes. John gives me a thumbs up and Adele mouths "I love you". JD wiping his eyes and my man back at my side whispers in my ear "You inspire me". *Crap the tears begin again!*

Mrs. Goldfarb back at the podium, she motions to Kevin and I to stay put. Ladies and Gentleman please have a seat. When I told you we brought out the big wigs this year, our next guest proves it. I would like to introduce an old and very dear friend to my husband and me, Jackson Durand. *Applause from the crowd and JD stands at the podium.*

*Whispering in my ea*r I knew you were special but tonight just showed me how special you are. *I'm kissed by JD* I had a conversation with this young lady *pointing to me* several months back. I wanted to know what type of work she did and from that question I learned so much. Then I inquired what could be done to improve awareness and support. In an instant with compassion in her voice, she outlined exactly what she would do. All the nuts and bolts, a detailed plan. Well young lady in partnership with Care House, to get you started…. Wait, Adele and John could you come up…. *Making their way to the stage, each of us even Kevin with puzzled looks* Beth in partnership with Care House I would like to introduce you to the future Amanda Yvonne Walker Community Center. *Behind us on a large screen sketches of the proposed plan and what it will offer.*

Adele, John and Kevin begin hugging one another. I release myself from Kevin's hold and hug and kiss JD ever so tightly. The crowd is on their feet. I whisper in JD's ear.... Something more you and your grandson have in common, you both actually listen and take stock in what I say. I love you JD and to name it after Kevin's mom, your one classy dude!

In this instant JD hugs me tighter "I love and adore you Beth". *The crowd begins to settle down. Adele hugs and kisses JD. Tears streaming down her face. Mrs. Goldfarb back at the podium.*

I can't think of any better way to end this evening. Wow.... JD.... Good night everyone and safe travels.

Chapter Eleven – Decisions

Beth, hey wakeup….. Beth

Kevin what time is it?

About seven…

How do you feel, do you feel ok?

Yes… Why? *Rolling over….*

Would you take a walk with me?

Kevin?

Please?

Yes I guess…..

Ten minutes later dressed in a pair of night shorts and top. At least I washed my face and brushed my teeth. Kevin where are we going?

Just follow me…… Please……

After about a ten minute walk, I see what has excited Kevin. A beautiful Gazebo covered in pink, yellow and white rose vines with snippets of ivy. The way the vines sit so comfortably and intertwined with one another their seasonal growth must be as old as this home. Eyeing this beauty I smell the impending summer air welcoming the unofficial mark of summer by way of this Memorial Day weekend.

Kevin?

I stumbled upon this beauty yesterday morning. My first thought was to have breakfast with my beautiful wife in the morning and then a romantic dinner with dancing under the moonlight in the evening.

Kevin it is beautiful!

Taking my hand, Kevin leads me up four stairs and onto the Gazebo where breakfast awaits.

Kevin…. This is beautiful…. But we have a house full of guest.

They will be okay. Between Cynthia and Mrs. Clarke everything will be perfect for them. *Pulling a seat out for me I sit and across from me Kevin sits.* Beth did I tell you how proud I am of you?

Yes you have and I love you for it. What about JD's surprise?

Amazing! Seems Adele and John loves it also.

Did you know about it?

Not at all. He took us all by surprise. But I guess your plate will be full in the coming months, setting up and running the Center!

Between that and a baby I don't know which will be more consuming.

I'm sure you will find the time. I just wish it wasn't in Brooklyn. Travel to and fro… Wait what did you say?

Kevin?

What did you say?

Between that and a baby I don't know which will be more consuming.

Beth *standing and almost knocking over the table and all its breakfast contents* you will consider having the baby?

No longer considering, you and I are having a baby!

Baby *choking back tears*

But wait Kevin, we have several challenges. Before we get excited let's meet with Dr. Warner. So not a word to anyone… Okay!

Beth okay, very okay. What changed your mind? *An alarm look* Beth I didn't pressure you did I?

Kevin you kept your word. I felt no pressure from you. What helped me with my decision is the love and support I feel from our family but more importantly you my dear husband.

Oh Beth…. *Hugging me* I so love you, baby I love you!

179

I know you do. You have never given me any reason to doubt you do. But remember, not a word to anyone until we know…

I promise.

I will call Dr. Warner and see if I can get in today. May not happen due to this being a holiday weekend.

Fine….. What time can we call?

Kevin!

Alright…..Alright… Up to a walk so you could see more of your property?

I would like that.

After at least a forty minute tour, Kevin and I are back at the house. Coming in through the kitchen we hear laughter and chatter from the dining room… Entering my heart is heavy and Kevin was right, between Cynthia and Mrs. Clark the table looks amazing.

Good morning everyone….

Wow you two were out and about early…

My loving husband had breakfast ready for me at six this morning. He found an old beautiful Gazebo on the grounds.

My grandson the romantic.

Adele you taught him well…. *And the room engulfs in laughter. I excuse myself and head up to my bedroom to make an appointment with Dr. Warner. Of course my loving husband right behind me.*

Beth is it too early to call?

No his office opens at eight …. Hello this is Beth Walker, I was hoping to get an appointment with Dr. Warner today?

Mrs. Walker Dr. Warner is booked for today. Is this an emergency?

Ah…. Not really I guess. How soon can he see me?

Wait, please hold.

Beth can they fit you in?

Probably not. I'm on hold

Hello Mrs. Walker Dr. Warner said he could see you at 11.

Great, thank you I will see you then.

Hanging up He can see me at 11.

Excited Get dress we have at least an hour drive.

What about our families?

Beth, everyone will find something to do!

Heading back downstairs

Beth where are you going?

To make sure everyone is okay?

You get dressed and I will confirm. I will also tell them we are going out for a bit.

Sighing okay Kevin…..

Arriving to Dr. Warner's office bout 10:30, I'm immediately given a cup for a urine sample. Once my deposit is made Kevin and I are ushered to an exam room where weight and blood pressure is taken and blood drawn. Handed a paper gown I quickly put it on and Kevin and I wait for Dr. Warner.

Baby are you okay?

Other than my butt hanging out I'm fine.

Just then Dr. Warner enters. Beth, Kevin how are you?

Hi Dr. Warner… You tell me how I'm doing

Well let's see. Lay back… come down, further… Okay that's good. Have you missed your period?

No…

How have you been feeling…?

I assumed I had the flu but it is going on good couple of weeks.

Well from what I gather from this end you've been suffering from the flu almost twelve weeks. I'm going to do a pelvic sonogram okay?

I guess *I look over to my husband who seems completely lost.*

Okay you will feel a little pressure…. Would you two like to hear your baby's heart beat?

What? Yes… *Kevin's expression…. Priceless*

Beth I would say almost twelve weeks. Everything looks good and a picture to start that baby book.

Thank you Dr. Warner

Get dressed and come to my office.

Dr. Jacob's leaves and Kevin seems frozen in place… Baby are you okay?

Tears forming in his eyes, other than meeting you this is one of my best days.

Awe… I love you Mr. Walker…

Baby…. *Kevin's voice cracking* I love you too *and I'm hugged and kissed.*

Knock….. Knock…..

Come in. Beth, Kevin have a seat. Everything looks good but Beth you have a lot of scarring and with your history we have to take some precautions.

Dr. Warner is Beth okay…. Is it safe for her to do this?

Yes… she is fine. But none of us can predict the future and it hasn't been a full twelve months since the last incident.

What about the heroine?

Yes part of the more recent trauma. I'm not concerned about the drug itself, it is out of your system, but you were injected with such high levels that it weaken your heart etc.

So what do we need to do?

For starters, no heroism… Understand! Avoid stress and listen to your body. Tired, stop what you're doing immediately. Pain call me. If unbearable call 911, go to the nearest hospital. I'm giving you a prescription for prenatal vitamins, folic acid and Beth your iron is very, very low. I'm going to put you on a prescription strength iron. If this doesn't raise your level, we may need to look at something more. And Just because of your history, sustain from sexual intercourse for the next two weeks. Just until you are in your second trimester at least until the fourteenth week.

As to your overall health and area of concern, I would like you to be seen by Dr. Monroe a cardiologist. You will be seen by me every two weeks and I would like Dr. Monroe's recommendations regarding how often you should be monitored by him. I'm assuming he too will suggest every two weeks. The only concern is your insurance, may not cover precautionary – preventive visits.

Dr. Warner, not an issue. Whatever you recommend for Beth we will do.

Well one other area, Beth your weight is a bit under. I assume because you had the "flu" *We all laugh* you haven't been able to keep anything down. So here's a prescription to help with the nausea. Any questions?

I'm sure we will once reality sinks in.

Kevin are you okay over there?

Dr. Warner no words….. I'm a happy man!

Well Beth, Kevin congratulations and I will see you in two weeks. Have Stacey schedule you to see Dr. Monroe. We will get you in for early next week.

Thanks Dr. Warner

Leaving Dr. Warner's office I note the endless smile on Kevin's face.

Kevin are you alright?

Baby I am more than alright in this moment I am the happiest man in the world but Beth, you do understand what Dr. Warner said.

Kevin?

I want to hear how you interpreted what Dr. Warner said to you in his office!

I heard him Kevin

I'm listening

Holy hell this is not how the next few months is going to go I won't push the limits…

Beth I need you to accept assistance. Mrs. Clarke can do the laundry, clean the house, our bedroom. I need you to let go of a lot of what you do.

Kevin I'm not just going to lay around on my ass okay!

No, I'm not saying that

Then lord…. What are you saying my loving husband?

I need you to promise me you will take it easy. Allow me, Mrs. Clark…. Allow us to take care of you for a change.

I promise

Say it again but this time uncross your fingers and toes…..

Baby you have my word, I promise! But Kevin you heard him, one day at a time okay?

Beth I'm trying my best not to shout to the universe how happy I am….. I'm trying my hardest to stay grounded, but baby you're having our baby.

Kevin….

Beth please let me just get this out before we get home…. Please!

Go ahead……

I'm going to be a dad…. Someone's father. *Pulling the car over onto the shoulder of the palisades Parkway*

Kevin what are you doing?

Taking my hand in his and looking me in the eyes Thank you *touching my stomach but in this moment Kevin's mood instantly changes*

Kevin are you alright? What's wrong?

Beth maybe you should stay with Adele and John in Alabama until …..

Oh no you don't Kevin. I'm not being shipped off like a package. Absolutely not. My home is here with you .No!

Beth….

No Kevin. I promised to abide by the rules and since the fire, the call I have, each and every one.

Throwing his hands to his face, now two of you are in danger.

Kevin stop!!!! I would rather have the Kevin from ten minutes ago who was a pain in the ass.

Beth, you just don't get it.

I get it Kevin. Now you're responsible for two. Well I can say the same. Do you know each and every time you leave for work I beg God to watch over you? When I don't hear from you by a certain time I have to talk myself out of a panic attack? And now if anything ever happened to you I will be raising a child all by myself. So stop this, we both worry.

Bear hugging me Beth I didn't realize. Baby I'm sorry.

Nothing to apologize for. It is what it is and knowing I have this special someone growing inside me, I will make sure my actions do not put either of us in danger.

That's all I ask for.

Great can we get going now, we still have a house full of people.

Beth should we say something?

Kevin????

Beth they all are here, the most important people in our lives.

Kevin what if…

Stop, every day is a "what if".

I guess, we are basically at the twelve week mark.

Thank you!!!! *and home we are headed.*

Arriving home, JD, Cynthia, Adele, John and Mrs. Clark are all in the kitchen.

Hey your back…

Yes we are. Why are all of you gathered here in the kitchen?

Beth I understand you not only purchased the table set here but you also put it together?

John, yes… Why?

Oh nothing really. I sat down to read the newspaper and drink a cup of coffee when all of a sudden the chair cracked and spilt in half.

Oh my God, are you okay?

Adele laughing One minute I saw my husband reading the paper next he was of the floor.

Oh John…

Beth I will never say you married my grandson for his money *and I am kissed by John.*

Listen, I purchased what I could afford. And nothing wrong with my table. Other than my office and bedroom, I furnished this complete house myself…. And proud to say put together most of what you see.

Don't look at me, I refused to be a part of it. Cynthia your sister is very pig headed.

You don't need to tell me twice.

Okay enough talking about me as though I'm not here. Shame on you *and I laugh.* Kevin you entertain our lovely family, I'm going up to change and to get your unborn child out of this toxic atmosphere. Talking about its mother this way.

The room goes completely silent, not a word from anyone. I make it to the top stair from the back staircase in the kitchen before I hear "Young lady get back here" The room erupts with congratulations and hugs.

Beth you stay we are coming up! Entering my bedroom I am followed by everyone.

I'm going to be a great-grandfather?

Hold it JD, we –you me and John will be great-grandparents and the three hug one another.

Cynthia pulls me to the side, Is everything okay? Are you okay?

Yes, so far all is fine. Talk later but will need to see a cardiologist next week. Just as a precaution. *In this moment my sister hugs me like no other time.*

You have too many people looking after you from heaven. All will be fine.

With you by my side….

Okay everyone a few things. Beth is to rest often and avoid stress.

Kevin!

I'm just repeating what Dr. Warner said.

Not exactly his words but for the next few weeks I will take it easy.

Beth, your health?

JD I'm fine, I promise. Just a few precautions due to my history.

Baby God is looking over you every second. Do not worry.

I'm not Adele. I'll leave that for your grandson *shaking my head to show my disapproval*

Beth anything you need I'm here, we all are here.

I know JD *looking at my support system I begin to cry*...

Beth…. Stop! *Kevin by my side*

Just happy tears…

Beth I never gave you and Kevin your wedding gift. Purchasing your home was to be my gift but my grandson wanted to do it on his own, for his bride *looking at Kevin* and I respect him for that. So from me to you and my future grandchild I would like to furnish your home.

JD it is furnished.

Hmm yes it is *said with total sarcasm* but we need steady furniture that can hold more than ten pounds. Our *looking at Adele and John* grandchild needs to be able to tap a piece of furniture without it coming apart. Please let me do this

Walking over to JD, You make it so difficult to say no. Thank you.

No young lady, thank you *and JD hugs me with tears in his eyes.* Alright time to celebrate. This is a wonderful surprise, dinner is on me. Come on Mrs. Clarke.

Grandfather you all go, I would like to spend some time with my wife and that little person tucked away.

I understand son. Alright I think a quick flight to Boston sounds like a great dinning idea. Let's get going.

Chapter Twelve – Birthday

Do you know who named you on this special day?

You did daddy...

Yes I did. I knew the name Elizabeth was the right name for my special girl.

Am I your special girl?

You certainly are.

Is Cynthia special?

Oh very special. Your big sister is my Satin Doll.... Anything ever happens to me your big sister will take care of you.

Nothing will ever happen to you daddy..... Right

Come on, today is your day...... My baby girl's birthday. Ready?

I'm ready daddy. Daddy I'm ready where are you? Daddy? Daddy?

Beth, wakeup....

Being shaken.... What Kevin?

Beth bad dream?

Hmm what time is it?

Almost four in the morning

Getting up

Beth where are you going?

Kevin you have another hour before you have to get up, I'm fine, go back to sleep!

Beth?

I'm just going down to the kitchen for something to drink.

Beth I'll get it

No go back to sleep.

Once in the kitchen I sit and try to clear my head. So much coming upon me all at once and I don't know how I am going to get through it. How am I going to deal? For starters this day. Last year, my day began with a special phone call promptly at 6 a.m. I recall the call as if it just happened. Rosie singing Happy Birthday to me.....

Beth today your birthday?

Yes it is little Miss. Rosie.....

Mama made you a cake *in the background Rosa saying* shh Rosie that's a surprise

Shh Beth that's a surprise. *Tears begin trickling down my face.*

So Beth Rosie and I will see you here at 6 as planned.

I will see you both then.

Okay. Wait Beth Rosie wants to say something

Beth can you come now?

No Rosie you have to go to school.

I can stay home?

No Rosie you have a big graduation to get ready for. Can you sing your graduation song?

I begin to live

Ha ha ha... No, we've only just begun to live?

Oh... Okay I'm going to school now. Bye Beth...

Bye my little love.

Inhaling deeply, Heavenly father help me through this day. I lay my head and rest upon the table.....

Beth, baby you've been down here all this time?

Huh... What time is it?

Beth what's going on with you?

Kevin *tears begin falling* just remembering last year this time. I spent my birthday with Rosie and Rosa and I have to say *my voice cracking* one of my best ones.

Oh, Beth... Baby!

Smiling Kevin I'm fine... Just memories

Rubbing my stomach And in a few months you can tell our little one all about Rosie....

Hmm...

Mrs. Clarke informed me you barely ate yesterday.

Kevin!

Don't Kevin me, are you feeling okay?

I am… Just nervous about today's visit with the cardiologist. I just want everything to be okay.

Baby it will but you must eat. It's been a week now since seeing Dr. Warner and the medication he prescribed for the nausea seems not to be working.

Kevin…. Let's get through today. If I still feel crappy I will make an appointment to see Dr. Warner.

So let's review today's plan.

Don't start Kevin

Beth!

Meeting Rochelle at noon in the City for lunch. Yes Donaldson will be with me. Then meeting you at Dr. Monroe's office at 3:00 p.m. But Mr. Walker I have a request…

I'm not liking where this is going.

It is my birthday and I want to go into the City in my own car, alone! Since receiving that beauty I can count on one hand the times I've driven it…

I'm not going to argue with you today. *Kissing me on the forehead.* I will see you at three.

Yup with bells on…..

Arriving at the restaurant about 12:15, I park and wait for Donaldson. With a nod, I head into the restaurant and Donaldson enters with me. Seeing Rochelle I am completely excited, I hug her completely.

Oh Rochelle……. I miss you *and tears begin to trickle down my face.*

Beth stop it, you're going to make me cry….

Both of us laughing Rochelle you look wonderful.

Beth you look tired but yet….. I don't know…

Oh Rochelle *and the tears begin again* I'm expecting.

((No))…. Oh my….. Beth I am so happy for you *hugging me tightly, then Rochelle realizes the events from last year. With a look of fright* Beth are you okay? Baby?

Laughing Yes I'm just tired *and the tears continue*

Taking my hand Come with me. *Entering the ladies room I become completely consumed by emotion.*

Beth…. what's going on?

Rochelle, I miss them so much…. And as the days get closer I think of them both more and more and I…. *I completely unravel*

Oh Beth *tears streaming down Rochelle's face* it's hard I know.

Both of them, Rosie and Rosa were killed because of me.

Taking me into her arms Stop this, do you hear me! None of this was your fault. And from this moment and for the sake of that baby *pointing to my stomach* stop the pity party. *Handing me a paper towel* Rosa and Rosie are with you every day.

Rochelle……

No, not hearing it. You did not do this. And I can't wait until the sick bastard that did is in custody so you can live again. But until that time, that baby needs you and only you. Do you understand?

Smiling and wiping my eyes I do

Good because I am starving…… Ready?

Walking hand in hand with my mentor, one of the two woman I look up to, we enter a private dining-room and to my surprise, my co-workers from Care House.

Catching up with my Care House Family the afternoon went very quick. Reminded of my next appointment by Donaldson I begin my goodbyes Everyone thank you for a wonderful, wonderful afternoon. I needed this but I have another appointment that I must get to.

But you haven't eaten anything, at least have a piece of cake.

No sorry... I haven't been feeling well..

Are you ... Your expecting aren't you?

Paige

Aren't' you?

Smiling I have to go...

Oh my god Beth

Paige stop hounding Beth.

Rochelle what do you know? You know something don't you?

Paige.... We will continue this conversation another time. Better yet, I would like to invite you all to my home for a small gathering in a few weeks..... I will email Paige all the information.

Beth I can't wait, will Detective Walker be home?

Paige.... When will your husband be back?

Not soon enough.... *and we all laugh...*

See you all very soon and thank you. *Hugging Rochelle I whisper* Thank you for today. I love you.

Beth I'm always here and I can't wait for my first God Child. I love you!

Thankfully my visit with Dr. Monroe went well. Already after five Kevin and I begin our trek home from the city. With Kevin driving the day begins to catch up with me and I find myself dozing off a bit.

Baby long day?

Yes I have to say a long one.

Beth I don't want you to be disappointed but I kept my word and didn't plan anything big for tonight. I didn't know how you would feel after your visit with Dr. Monroe.

I'm glad it's over. I feel relieved hearing I'm doing well from Dr. Monroe.

Baby so am I. But he reminded you to take it easy.

I know Kevin, right now I look forward to going home, taking off my clothes and enjoying my beautiful backyard you so graciously got for me.

Do you have an appetite yet?

You know I actually do….

Then what should we get?

Just hear me out, I would love a White Castle cheeseburger and onion rings.

Oh Beth…. That sounds….

Yummy!

From no appetite to White Castle, I'm a bit afraid but whatever you desire.

Stopping at White Castle Kevin orders enough food for an army. We arrive home approximately fifteen minutes later and I immediately go up and change my clothes to an old pair of sweat shorts and a tank.

Beth are you changed yet? Are you coming down?

Yelling back Coming now. *Making my way back downstairs I enter the kitchen where I see Mrs. Clark suppressing a smile,* Mrs. Clark everything okay?

Yes Beth. How did your medical appointment go?

Everything is fine, both of us are doing okay. Did Kevin go outside yet?

He certainly did. He ask that you follow the trail of rose petals…

This man…. Thank you *following the rose petal path, I end at a boat docked? The same boat from the island????*

Beth, you're probably not up to sail but I thought for tonight we could enjoy dinner and a movie on board.

Kevin does this boat belong to you?

Well my grandfather and I. We purchased it together about six years ago.

Wow!!! *Making my way to the top deck I'm amazed* How in the hell did you make White Castle look like a catered meal?

The magic of Mrs. Clarke. But also know if the White Castle doesn't sit well, I had Mrs. Clark make her famous chicken noodle soup. And if not in the mood for soup *taking a lid off another silver server* your favourite Penne ala Vodka.

Wow Mr. Walker.

And after dinner turning me around, a movie under the stars….

What movie?

The one and only Elvis Presley and GI Blues!

((KEVIN REALLY))

Really, have a seat..

After my wonderful dinner Kevin and I stretch out on a double lounger. On the big screen my one and only Elvis Presley. Unfortunately although one of my favourites, today's stretch in the city caught up with me and I find myself falling asleep.

Awaken by the need to go to the bathroom, I find Kevin in an animated conversation with Thomas.

Hey you two everything okay?

It is Beth….. Are you going in?

I was to use the bathroom… Kevin what's wrong?

Beth nothing for you to worry about!

Kevin keeping it from me will make me worry more!

Michael stopped by Cynthia's home earlier today.

For what?

He was intoxicated. Demanding to see you to wish you a happy birthday.

Cynthia okay?

Luckily your nephews were over. They handled the situation and sent him on his way.

Shit they didn't do anything to be arrested for?

No, not that I know of. But Beth I'm adding a detail to Cynthia just for a few days.

Cynthia okay with that?

Yes she is. Whatever occurred over there today has her a bit uneasy.

I'll call her to come up.

I tried that, she refused.

I'll call her. Baby I'll meet you in the house. Good night Thomas.

Good night Mrs. Walker and by the way Happy Birthday.

Thank you!!!

Entering the house I call Cynthia immediately

Hey Cynthia.

Happy Birthday

Thank you.... But I'm calling about Michael.

Beth something is wrong with him and his mother. I called that woman to let her know her son was at my home looking for you intoxicated and she did not find anything wrong with it.

Cynthia I'm sorry.

Beth what are you sorry for? You didn't do anything and you don't need to worry, Kevin is handling it.

I would feel better if you came up here and stayed a few days....

I can't do that and I'm fine. So enjoyed your birthday?

I did.......

How did your appointment go?

Same recommendation as Dr. Warner. Rest, take an easy etc…

Are you doing that?

I am. But before I forget, I invited a few people from work to come up, probably the end of the month for a small gathering. Can you and the boys come up?

We should but Beth what happened to resting?

Cynthia don't worry…..

Alright Elizabeth

Oh no, time for me to hang up. I'll give you a call tomorrow. I love you.

Love you too. Talk in the morning.

By the time I end my call, Kevin enters our room with a rather large box in hand.

Mr. Walker what is in the box?

Well I couldn't resist, so please open the box?

Opening the box I find a rather large stuffed bear Kevin I thought we weren't getting anything until we are all clear.

Well the bear needed a home.

A six foot bear?

Do you notice the bear's ears?

Sapphire earrings?

Happy Birthday baby….

Kevin they are absolutely beautiful. Thank you!

Well when we get the clear to resume activities, I would love to see you in them.

I can put them on now?

Oh no baby.... I want you completely nude with just the sapphire earrings...

Really Mr. Walker.... *Smiling*....

Oh baby really! But for now, could I ask that you lay in my arms?

I can't think of any other way to end my birthday. I love you and thank you for today.

Chapter Thirteen – Past and Present

Good Morning you two, I'm here. The weather is perfect, only going up to 80 degrees today. That's hot enough for me. Hopefully a shower will come along this evening. The season is coming in so strong we are beginning to see drought conditions already. But enough about me, how are you? Hmm look at this place, *brushing leaves away* let's get this place cleaned up a bit. I came with surprises. Oh don't say I shouldn't have, I had to. Rosa a bouquet of beautiful roses. This time I mixed the colors to give you a variety. And for you my little love, how could I come see you without bringing Hello Kitty and Barbie *resting the roses, Hello Kitty and Barbie against the headstone.* What a beautiful summer morning…. Rosa I know you're asking why I came so early… Well I'm sure you two will be visited by many today, I wanted to be alone here with you.

I guess you both already know, a baby is on the way. Who would have ever guessed? *With a chuckle* if it wasn't for you my little love, knowing how much happiness you gave me *tears begin to escape* I don't know if I would consider this. But from the moment you entered this world you gave me something to look forward to every second of the day. Coming here this morning I drove by your old apartment. I didn't go in, just sat out front for a few minutes. I did however get a glimpse of Mr. Jackson and that young woman you say frequents him early in the morning while his wife is at work. *Laughing* and your suspicion Rosa of he being a she, I do think I saw an Adam's apple. Oh and Rosa you will be happy to know the community garden is back up and running. I don't know who is managing you and Rosie's plot but someone is

That someone is me.

Completely taken off guard I jump and nearly pee myself Jasmine?

Laughing Beth I didn't mean to frighten you.

Laughing I'm okay *and I hug Jasmine*

Beth I guess you and I had the same idea, come early?

Yes I guess we did. How are you?

Doing okay Beth, You?

Okay, doing okay. Still putting in those long hours?

Most days even longer. But something good has come out of it.

And what might that be?

Raising her left hand to display her ring finger

Congratulations Jasmine.

Thank you.

Set a date yet?

Probably spring of next year.

Well congratulations!

What about you Beth?

I begin to cry I told myself I wasn't going to cry *laughing* but I should have known better. *Trying with great difficulty from falling apart* I should have been the one not them. You two are gone because of me. I will never forgive myself. I miss you two every day of my life. It should have been me taken away not you two. *I weep uncontrollably.* I will never forgive myself. Never.

Beth do not blame yourself, you didn't do this!

I didn't do it but it is because of me.

Beth Ro and Rosie wouldn't want you like this.

I just miss them both. I'm sorry...

Beth don't be. You gave my sister and niece a life neither would have had if you weren't in their lives. No one deserves dying as they did but in life you gave both of them a life, a life neither would have had. You stuck by my sister knowing… You never let her and Rosie's health stop you from doing anything with them or for them and for that I will be forever grateful.

But it is because of me they are not able to share in your wedding, Rosie plying with friends. All this, being here right now is because of me. *In this very moment I completely break down. In this moment I hear a familiar comforting voice*

Beth… Baby get up

Kevin I'm okay. *Rising to my feet* Jasmine I'm very sorry. *I walk as quickly as I can to my car, Kevin right behind me. Once to my car an overwhelming feeling hits. I begin vomiting over and over again. Attempting to stand upright, I double over from an excruciating pain in my abdomen area.*

Beth what's wrong?

Attempting to rise to an upright position the pain hits again. In a flash I'm positioned in the car with Kevin in the driver seat.

Kevin…. I'm alright

……………………

Kevin please slow down

…………………..

211

((Kevin))

No response until we arrive at Long Island Jewish Hospital. Stopping exactly in front of the emergency entrance Kevin swoops me up and carries me in. Immediately taken into an exam area I hear the nurse talking to Kevin

Sir whose blood? Are you hurt?

Hearing the question I look up to Kevin who in this moment wants to be brave but his eyes begin to water. I shake my head no and mouth "I'm sorry"…. I close my eyes and in seconds all is peaceful. I drift into a slumber.

Hey what time is it?

8:30 in the morning

I've been sleep for over 24 hours?

You have

And you've been here all this time holding my hand?

Baby where else am I to be?

Kevin's words hit me like a ton of bricks Kevin I'm sorry, I promise we will try again *I begin to cry*

Beth you and the baby are fine.

Really? Then what was wrong?

For starters you're severely dehydrated.

What about the bleeding?

Not sure but our little person here *touching my stomach* has a strong heartbeat and doing just fine.

Kevin thank you…. But ah when can we go home?

Dr. Warner will be by this morning to check on you.

You didn't tell anyone about this did you?

Oh my beautiful wife expect an ear full.

Knock….. Knock….

Come in

You're up

Good morning Dr. Warner

Good Morning Dr. Warner

How are you feeling?

Much better…

Any pain?

No…

Well Beth it seems you have been doing everything I suggested you not do.

Dr. Warner… I've been trying

Beth you need to try harder. I want to see you again in a week. Your blood pressure was elevated.

Before prescribing anything I want to see how the next few days go.

Okay…

And Beth, if the nausea continues call me immediately.

I will. Thank you …..

See you in week and complete bed rest until I see you. Do you hear me?

Don't worry Dr. Warner Beth will have no choice but to adhere to your instructions!

Looking at Kevin I present with a somewhat pissed expression.

See you two next week.

Preparing myself for the ride of my life Kevin and I head home. From Little Neck to the George Washington Bridge, no conversation. He's holding my hand, smiled at me several times but no comments about yesterday.

Beth how are you feeling?

Fine?

Okay!

Kevin I know you have something to say about yesterday, please can we have this debate and get it over with?

Beth, what is there for me to say?

How did you know I was at the cemetery?

Beth I know the date, remember I was there. I can understand the need to go to the grave site. What I don't understand was your need to sneak out and not tell anyone. Mrs. Clarke was very worried when she went up to check on you and you weren't in bed.

I know it was foolish. And if I didn't thank you before, thank you for checking up on me. If you weren't there who knows what the outcome would have been.

Kissing my hand Beth just promise me you're done.

Kevin I have a request. I would like to go away for a few days, maybe to Alabama?

Sweetheart I know the dates. Flying probably not a good idea. I can call Dr. Warner but I doubt he will give an approval.

I told a few people from work I was planning a gathering and wanted them to come up. I would like to set the date for the end of the month.

Beth you're supposed to be resting.

I know, but

Listen I understand, it sounds like a great idea. But you will not lift a finger. If you can agree on that then we have a plan. And I will request the week off. You and I will occupy each other.

Or kill one another.

Ha ha, Mrs. Walker but I think we have a plan!

Kevin….. Thank you.

Beth baby I'm doing what I am supposed to do. Nothing here above and beyond. Just my husbandly duties….

Hmmm I wonder what my wifely duties are *laughing*

Well once this little person is safely in this world we will explore further your wifely duties.

Kevin with Gods guidance that will be four months from now plus recovery period. I cannot wait that long. We will see what Dr. Warner says next week but until then I hope you're open to some creative alternatives.

Completely taking Kevin by surprise Elizabeth Walker!

Chapter Fourteen – Goodbye to the Old

Kevin….. Kevin…… Kevin wake up

Startled Beth what's wrong?

Placing Kevin's hand on top of my lower abdomen

No…. No way, he or she is moving….

I know…. *My eyes begin to swell* this makes it so real…. Kevin, we are having a baby.

Taking me into his arms Yes we are. Wow and it seems he is a kicker.

He? *Laughing*

He or she I am blessed to have either. When did it start?

About four this morning… Started as a flutter then it got a little stronger. *I begin to cry..*

Beth, sweetheart what's wrong? This is a good thing.

Kevin just thinking back, the baby I was carrying I never experienced this and at the time - at the time I was a bit further along.

Beth don't……

Kevin I've come to terms with it. But…. more recently I think about what could have been.

Beth I know you believe in God.

Of course I do.

Well maybe our heavenly father made a decision for you.

Kevin I don't follow

Who knows if that baby would have been healthy or not. The damage done to you over ten years ago impacts your health and the health of this one year to date. I read between the lines when Dr. Warner talked about the recent incident vs. the previous incident.

I know Kevin.

Did you just feel that?

I've been feeling it since 4 a.m. *and I smile*

Well that's our little someone telling you I'm here mom and can't wait to see you.

Smiling I hope that's true

Baby it is and from this day on, we are going to get ready for this little person. No more what if's ok?

Yes....

And I think it is time you and Cynthia go shopping...

Shopping for what?

Baby I know you don't think so, but your clothing is a bit tighter and last night I thought I was seeing things but baby you are beginning to show.

No not your imagination, I am and not just a little *laughing* I seemed to have popped.

Well what I saw, what I see baby you are absolutely beautiful.

Did I tell you I loved you yet?

Nope...

I love you Mr. Walker, *climbing on top of Kevin Ready?*

Beth!

Kevin last night was wonderful. But we have to make up for lost time.

Beth?

Dr. Warner gave us the go ahead.... So...

Beth Dr. Warner just gave his approval

Over a week ago *taking my tee shirt and boxer shorts off* I AM READY*!*

Beth are you sure?

Kevin, this is how sure I am *I begin kissing Kevin on his mouth. I then move my way to his neck and ears.*

Beth.....

Kevin *pulling his shorts off* I want you to kiss me here *pointing to my neck* then here *my breast* then here *my inner thigh*... I then want you to enter me very very slowly and once comfortably in, remain completely still and allow me to do any and all movement.

Is that all you're asking for?

Baby it is….

I've told you many times before, I am here to please my wife.

Kissing me I begin my climb to heavenly bliss.

I want to welcome all of you to our home today. Many of you are aware of what this date means. *Kevin holding my hand tighter.* Last year, more specifically June and July of last year presented some of the most horrific times of my life. Two people who meant the world to me were taken away very tragically then *my voice cracking* I was abducted and left for dead. For five days I was missing from my love ones, my sister and nephews. From the people I work with - *smiling* my work family and from my then very handsome future husband *with swollen eyes* who knew. But I was found... Found by two wonderful men. My now husband who never gave up and his partner – Erickson. This day marks my being found. But this day also marks so much more. At four this morning for the first time I felt my baby move.

At five I woke my very tired husband to share in the experience and in that moment I saw the love he not only has for me but for this little person tucked away. It was this morning I decided to no longer acknowledge this date as the date I was saved but rather the day I felt my baby move for the first time. The day I gathered with family and friends to officially announce I'm going to be a mom. *Smiling* I'm going to be a mom. The day my husband very carefully told me I was beginning to show. This is what this day means to me now. I will no longer acknowledge what happened one year ago. Unfortunately I will have the memories forever but I will no longer allow these memories to dictate how I am to be. So please help me by raising your glass and toast to relinquishing the original meaning of today and replacing it with the memories made from this morning on.

Kevin taking me into his arms I love you baby...

But I love you *more Erickson pulling me from Kevin's hold then hugging me.*

Wow where were you guys when I was looking for a date?

Look no further, I'm next in line.

Erickson didn't you come with a date?

Winking at me yes but Beth I will dump her in a second if you say the word.

Laughing Erickson you say that now but when I'm about 200 pounds into my pregnancy you will only toss me aside.

Kevin shaking his head Erickson go find your date before I give her an ear full.

Beth see how I'm treated

Kissing Erickson on the cheek Always the victim *and I laugh.* Sweetheart going to my work family *laughing,* you handle yours. *Walking away I hear Kevin and Erickson laughing.*

Hey guys I hope you're eating? A lot of food!

Beth we are. But we are more stunned by your home. Wow....

Paige thank you.

Can we have a tour?

Sure...

Follow me.

Wait, what bout Rochelle?

Rochelle has been here several times already. She lives nearby.

Oh okay *as if insulted?*

Starting upstairs I give Paige, Pam and Daphne a tour.

Beth which will be the nursery?

We are thinking about knocking a wall out and adjoining our room with this one.

Wow....

So should we head back down?

Around 9 p.m. the party dwindles down to Erickson and his date, Rochelle and her husband, Paige and Cynthia.

So Beth, when is the due date?

Before I can answer I hear JD's voice?

Yes when should I expect my great - grandchild?

JD? Adele and John? What are you doing here? *I rush to each and bear hug all.*

We came to support our granddaughter and see how you are doing.

Crying I think you know everyone here. *Hugging JD, Adele and John again*

Kevin..... You knew they were coming?

I did. But due to the hurricane they couldn't fly out until late this afternoon.

So Beth, due date?

Official due date December 20th.

A Christmas baby, Oh Beth

Well I hope this means all grandparents will be here for the Holidays?

Beth John and I will be here with Bells on.

Winking at JD I know probably not on the exact Holiday JD but I hope during.

I will be here in an instant. My goal is to be here when my great grand-child comes into this world.

Between the four of you, this child is one blessed kid.

No Beth we are the blessed ones…..

Okay enough of the wet eyes, grandfather, John, Jeff and Erickson on board "the boat" *smiling at me* I have a perfectly aged bottle of Scotch that I was saving for a special occasion. Follow me.

Looking at Adele smiling You know your grandson doesn't drink.

Adele laughing Beth I know. *Kissing me* You make my grandson so happy.

Adele he does the same for my sister

Ladies I need to excuse myself.

Beth could you direct me to the bathroom?

Laughing Sure I'm going to the same place.

Walking in Paige stops me, JD Durand is Kevin's grandfather?

Yes Paige. But it isn't something we talk about and you are among the few that knows and I need you to keep it to yourself.

I understand. Alright, bathroom please.

With everyone not staying the night gone, Adele, Cynthia and Mrs. Clarke begin cleaning up. JD, John and Kevin off in what seems like a deep conversation.

Beth what are you doing?

Cynthia I'm helping.

You relax, we have this. Plus the caterers cleaned up the majority.

Cynthia…

Beth don't start…

Alright, alright. Kissing Cynthia then Adele I'm going in. If you see my other half let him know…. I love you two…. See you in the morning.

Good night Beth.

Chapter Fifteen – When It Rains It Pours

Rochelle do you think a November 1st ribbon cutting is doable?

Beth and Kevin absolutely. I will coordinate with the Mayor's office and get the press release out immediately.

I can't believe in two months this place will be open. *Turning to Kevin* You and your grandfather what you two have done here in such a short amount of time is amazing.

Yes the two of you are truly a dream team. Which brings me to my next question, what about the clinical director position, Beth have you filled it?

Well I was waiting for the right time to ask the right person?

Presenting somewhat disappointed Oh any leads?

I have someone in mind but not sure if this person is willing to give up a very public position to take on a position here.

Smiling Well Mrs. Walker maybe if you posed the question to this individual you might just be surprised by his or her answer.

Ladies I consider myself to be a somewhat patient man but you two in this moment.

Then to put you out of your misery Mr. Walker, I would like to apply for the position.

Apply? Really Rochelle! I would love for you to take the position but Rochelle not just clinical director but Co. Executive Director?

You're kidding me right?

No you and me if you accept? But you know we will be working for peanuts.

I would be truly honored.

Hugging Rochelle I can't wait. But *looking down at my watch* I wanted to stop by Ms. Black's before heading home. I better get going.

Beth are you up to the drive?

I will have to be. I'm the one who wanted to drive myself down today.

You do have a choice baby. I need to go back to the precinct but I will meet you and either Donaldson or Thomas will drive my car home.

Are you sure?

To have you all to myself, I'm very sure.

Well I'm sure of one thing, Kevin you need to rub off onto my husband.

We all laugh. Rochelle could we meet next week to go over few things?

Actually Beth I'm off a few days next week to get the kids off to school for the first week. How about meeting Tuesday? A new spa recently opened right in town. I could make all the arrangements?

Looking over to Kevin for a sense of approval before I agree. With a smile Sounds great.

Alright until then Kevin – Beth thank you.

No thank you. See you Tuesday. *Departing from Rochelle Kevin and I walk to my car.* Alright Mr. Walker I'm off too. See you in about forty-five minutes?

Yes *kissing me....* Did I tell you how beautiful you look today?

Looking like a baby orca, if you did you would be telling a lie.

Baby if you only knew your beauty. You are more beautiful this very moment then the first day I laid my eyes on you and that day you took my breath away.

How did I ever get so lucky? See you in a few *and I am on my way to Ms. Black's.*

After circling Ms. Black's building at least five times I finally find a space on Flatbush. Thomas double parks on the side of me and Donaldson steps out immediately to assist me. I'll make this quick looking down at my ever so growing belly, you're giving your mom a run for her money today. Stepping out of the car I make my way to the trunk. This is one day I won't debate with Donaldson regarding his assistance. Today it will be greatly appreciated

Are you feeling well Mrs. Walker?

A long day and a wee bit tired. The sooner we deliver these things the sooner we can get home.

Not a problem Mrs. Walker. But if you like I can deliver them for you.

No I'm excited to see her kids but thank you for the offer.

Then please allow me to carry the items.

No argument today *and as Donaldson and I unload the items from my trunk I hear a voice that sends a cold chill through my body. Looking to my left a face to match that voice.*

Mrs. Morris I thought it was you. How are you?

Mrs. Walker and I am doing well.

Donaldson no longer bending into the trunk stands to an upright position to see who I am talking to. No longer presenting in that somewhat friendly mood, the look on his face confirms who is in our presence. Dropping the items back into the trunk he closes the trunk and takes a few steps to my side which allows for a full body view of me. The look on Michael's face turns to one that I come to know too well.

Mrs. Walker huh. Excuse me *extending his hand* you must be Mr. Walker and by the looks of things a soon to be father!

Michael he's a friend of mine and we are late for an appointment.

Friend huh! And you can't or won't give me a few minutes of your precious time?

The time bomb ticker is about to strike Donaldson I would rather head home. Michael take care of yourself.

Grabbing for my arm Donaldson immediately puts himself in the way, shoving me a bit and I now have Thomas taking me by the arm.

What the fuck is the problem man?

Sir Mrs. Walker will not engage in any further conversation. Enjoy your day.

Beth who are these clowns? Could I please talk to you for a second?

Michael

Please

Stepping forward a bit, I eye both Thomas and Donaldson an approval look. I step forward and is eye to eye with Michael.

Can I speak with you privately?

No Michael

Well how have you been?

Kevin, the past year is what it is.

Beth I'm really sorry for what happened.

I'm sorry to hear about your wife. I hope your coping?

I am.

Have you heard from your girls?

Of course I have.

So they are no longer missing?

Anger surfacing upon his face What? Who?

Laughing

Michael you've been drinking?

No… no why?

Because you reek of alcohol.

Nah.

Michael what are you doing in Brooklyn? New York in general? Did you move back?

Laughing No I came to see my mother.

Well I'm a bit tired and going to be on my way.

Tired, huh pregnancy and driving a BMW. Life must be fucking fantastic for you.

Michael enjoy the rest of your day *turning on my heel I feel myself falling against my car front forward, shoved with force with words I've become too familiar with* Bitch don't turn your back on me. *In this moment Thomas leaps from my side and knocks Michael to the ground. Donaldson helps me to my feet*

Mrs. Walker are you okay?

I am *tears begin to fall.* Let's just go *but my suggestion completely ignored and this encounter just got worse, Kevin and Ericson arrive*

Beth are you okay?

I am. Let's just go home

In a second. Thomas why the need to have Mr. Morris on the ground?

Mr. Walker He forcefully shoved Mrs. Walker as well as being verbally insultive.

Kevin's expression goes from "I'm going to give you the benefit of the doubt" to "you just fucked up" look.

Donaldson please take my wife home.

The only way I am going home is if you are with me so let's go.

Beth please I beg you, please go with Donaldson

I've never seen this level of anger coming from Kevin. Erickson by his side coaching him to take me home.

Everyone please, step the fuck away from me. Beth please I beg you, go home. Donaldson take her home now.

On his feet now, Michael brings himself eye to eye with Kevin So you're the new husband huh.

Fearful of what is about to happen I step in between Kevin and Michael. Taking Kevin's hand I attempt to grasp his attention and succeed by breaking his stare. With Kevin's hand in mine we begin to walk toward the passage side of the car.

Beth take care of yourself and I hope that baby your carrying doesn't end up like ours.

His words practically shatters me. Falling to pieces from within tears begin to fall fast. I turn for Kevin and he is no longer by my side but rather pinning Michael by the throat against the car.

Did you just threaten my wife? Did you?

....

You're a sick - sick individual. Your child didn't make it into this world at your own hand. And all these years later what your sick fucking ass did affects my child's development and my wife's health. *Ericson, Donaldson and Thomas all trying unsuccessfully to pull Kevin off.*

Kevin let him go, please. He's drunk Kevin and probably doesn't know what he is saying *although deep down inside I know he meant every word. The alcohol just giving him encouragement.*

After several minutes the two are separated. Kevin taking my hand turns to Erickson Do not allow this sick bastard behind the wheel. I suggest taking him in and allow him to sleep it off. *Although we all hear Kevin's instructions the eye exchange between him and Erickson presents as a language of its own that only the two understands. With nothing further to say*

Kevin motions me to get into the car. Kevin now in the driver seat we begin for home.

Baby are you okay *squeezing my hand?*

I am

And what about our special someone *said as Kevin rubs my stomach. The physical affection sparks my unraveling. Kevin pulls to the side of the road and instantly hugs me completely.*

I'm okay….. Just want to get home.

After about an hour on the road Kevin and I arrive home.

Baby can I get you anything?

Trying to hold back tears No Kevin I just want to lay down

Can I join you?

With tears falling now I would love that.

From my words instantly Kevin takes my hand into his and leads the way to our bedroom. Upon entry Kevin guides me to our bed and assist with taking my shoes off. Pulling one of his oversized tee shirts that I wear very often from his drawer and a pair of boxer underwear I too have claimed as my own but worn only when he isn't home. I'm dressed completely in my favorite comfort clothing. His familiarity of me again heavies my heart and the flood gates open. Kevin takes me into his arms and we lay in bed in complete silence with the only source of light peeking in through the drawn blinds. Feeling my safest as always in Kevin's arms I dismiss the many questions dancing in my head regarding why Michel is in New York, Brooklyn. I refuse to give in to his accusation of my killing my child. I instead remind myself of all my blessings. I close my eyes and easily fall sleep.

Approximately around three in the morning I'm wakened by my baby's moment. Instantly rubbing my stomach I smile. Turning to my side to look at my husband to my surprise he isn't here? I get up and check the bathroom no Kevin. I go downstairs first checking the kitchen, library and the reminder of the first floor. I head back to my room to grab my robe. Passing the nursery entrance from within our bedroom I see Kevin sitting in the rocker.

Hey are you okay?

Beth did I wake you?

No this little person did *touching my stomach*

You didn't eat this evening!

No I didn't..... I will get something now. But why are you sitting here in the dark?

Reminding myself of all my blessings. You and *taking my hand to pull me closer*, this little person here. *Unable to maintain his composure Kevin buries his head into my stomach and breaks down.*

Kevin stop this.

Beth I saw him put his hands on you. I saw it with my own eyes.

Kevin I'm fine, your baby is fine. Stop!

Beth I've never been a person, a man to wish or want harm to come to anyone but today I found myself wanting to end this man's life.

Kevin he's a broken man. He is living in his hell.

You continue to amaze me.

You shouldn't be amazed. You got me to this level of letting go. You instilled my belief in "real love".

Guiding me to sit on his lap Kevin I do have one question.

Yes he is still in holding.

And your reason for bringing him in is to find out what he was doing in Brooklyn?

My little Nancy Drew. Enough of this. Would you like to something to eat before or after?

With an extra-large smile, of course after. *Kissing my husband we are interrupted by Donaldson's voice.*

Mr. Walker? Mr. Walker sir?

Stepping out of the nursery Donaldson what is it?

Sorry to interrupt sir but Charles needs to speak with you urgently *handing Kevin his cell phone.*

Charles?

....

I can't fly to Texas after today.

....

Interrupting Kevin what happened?

Charles I will call you right back.

Kevin handing Donaldson back his phone. Please tell Thomas to stand by

Yes sir *and Donaldson leaves*

Kevin what's wrong?

Inhaling deeply JD had a heart attack...

Is he ok? Kevin?

He's in surgery right now

Okay let's go.

Beth you can't fly and I'm not leaving you here.

Kevin I'm going with or without you *immediately beginning to dress*

Beth the baby

Will be fine. We both will be fine!

Picking up his phone to call I assume Charles

Okay set it up. Beth and I will be ready in about an hour. *Kevin hangs up. He walks to* the edge of the bed and sits.

I walk over Are you okay?

Baby I should be asking you that.

If you haven't noticed yet I am always okay, more than okay in your presence. Now for once let me look after you.

Taking me completely into his arms I love you baby so much.

I know you do.

And this person here, let's get some food into you before we do anything else. You get dressed and I will make you a sandwich.

I would like that.

Chapter Sixteen – When Family is not Family and Strangers Are

Now five in the morning Kevin, Mrs. Clarke, Thomas, Donaldson and I fly out of a private heliport located right here in Rockland county. The plan set in motion is to take this twenty minute flight to JFK then transfer to JD's private plane which is ready to go. Keeping my eyes completely shut, Kevin squeezes my hand. I can't wait to land. I assume my little attachment feels the same because his or her movement is very intense.

Arriving to JFK finally we are escorted to another private hanger where a familiar face stands waiting.

Devlin nice to see you again.

Yes but I wish it was under better circumstances *turning to Kevin* Sorry to hear about your grandfather.

Thanks man.

And by the looks of things congratulations to both of you.

Thanks.

Boarding the plane Kevin insures everyone is on-board and confirms departure. Once in the air Kevin reviews the plan Charles put into place.

Beth Mrs. Clarke has extended her home to us and we will be staying with her.

Looking over to Mrs. Clarke to thank her I notice a look of worry and concern. Just staring out of the window.

When we arrive, we will head directly to the hospital and Mrs. Clarke will be taken to her home. But Beth I must forewarn you, Charles confirmed the media is everywhere.

Okay but they don't know who you are, right?

Beth many years ago it came out JD had a biracial grandson. It didn't last long but it came out. Times like this the media has a way of bringing up issues from the past.

Seeing the uneasy look on Kevin's face Baby what has you so worried?

The press finding out about you, me and especially the baby. We don't need that type of attention. Not now.

Kevin stop worrying, it will work out *laying my head on his shoulder* I'm going to take a nap.

Rubbing my belly Do you want something to eat?

No thanks, a nap is all I need. *I'm kissed, my bottom rubbed and where Kevin's hand remains.*

After about a three hour flight we finally arrive to Houston Medical Center. I take notice of the Mayhem Charles warned us of, reporters and news cameras camped out at all the entrances. Following Kevin's lead we head in unnoticed by all. Charles discreetly meeting us at the elevator he debriefs Kevin of what is going on. Allowing for privacy I walk down to where I assume is JD's room based on security outside the door. Upon entering I am stopped.

Excuse me ma'am only immediate family. *Before I could answer Donaldson by my side confirms my identity and I am allowed into the room.*

Not knowing what I'm about to encounter I say one last internal prayer then enter the room. To my surprise JD is sitting up scrolling through the channels but his appearance saddens me. Looking frail and with so many apparatuses attached to him.

What are you doing sitting up?

What on earth are you doing here?

I heard someone very near and dear to me had a heart attack *hugging JD tightly*

I did but the good lord rejected me *we both laugh.* Come here and sit, get off your feet.

JD I'm fine but you on the other hand.

Beth nothing in this world is going to keep me from seeing my great grandchild.

How are you feeling?

Much better now that you are here. But please tell me you didn't come all this way by yourself?

No your grandson is with Charles.

He came?

Yes he did. Your grandson loves you.

Tearing I know he does. The one person I've done so much wrong to...

Stop it your grandson does not feel that way.

Beth you

Interrupting JD I see how you are with Kevin and I can't wait to see you with your great-grandchild in a few months. But in order for you to be around in a few months you sir must take care of yourself and allow others to look after you.

Beth I'm going to try.

I need more than a try sir *and I kiss JD on his forehead. But just in this moment I hear a woman's voice questioning who I am.*

Jackson one of your whores?

Excuse me*? A bit amused by the allegation*

Your excused, please leave..... Excuse me *talking to security* please escort this whore from my husband's room and insure she does not return.

Blanche

Standing to face this woman, my noticeable expansion catches her attention

A pregnant whore at that. You never Surprise me. Who knew you could still get an erection!

Blanche this is Kevin's wife!

....

I'm Elizabeth Walker not a whore, not an escort nor a prostitute. *Just then Kevin and Charles bolts into the room.*

Beth is everything okay?

Oh it is. I was just introducing myself to Blanche is it?

Blanche staring intensely at me, more so my belly. Her stare intense, long and hard.

Blanche *JD attempting to grasp her attention*

.... Jackson do you think having all these people here is good for you?

Blanche please don't do this.

Grandfather I'm going to get Beth settled in. I will be back later this evening.

Kevin don't go. Blanche please.

Kissing JD We will be back later today. Get some rest. And we both love you.

Taking my hand into his I'm very sorry and I love the three of you....

Kevin's demeanor presents with both sadness and anger. But I assume his grasping of his grandfather's hand and squeezing it is his way of expressing his love and concern in this moment. Taking my hand he walks completely pass Blanche without batting an eye and lead us out to the hallway. But the smartass I am I can't leave without having somewhat of a final word. I release myself from Kevin's hold and re-enter JD's room.

Ah Excuse me, Blanche I wouldn't want to make this any more uncomfortable for either of us so I'm planning to return about three. Would that be okay for you?

I'm sure my stay will be done by 3.

Wonderful. I hope we have another opportunity to meet again. *Looking over to JD he mouths thank you and smiles.* Take care Blanche *and I exit the room.*

In the hall Charles, Donaldson, the gentleman securing JD's room and Kevin are all smiling at me.

Did I miss something?

No put apparently Charles and I did.

Huh?

Taking my hand Nice to know you're not JD's whore!

Ha Ha... *In a whisper* But I am yours - chef in the kitchen, a lady in the living room, a mother to your soon to be child and a whore in the bedroom.

Kevin completely surprised by my statement stops short.

Elizabeth Lillian Cook – Walker!

Would you want it any other way?

Baby *shaking his head.*

Good! And by the way we need to finish what was started early this morning

Beth you continue to surprise me!

Arriving to Mrs. Clarke's home I am absolutely stunned by the picture perfect property.

Kevin Mrs. Clarke must really love you.

Why do you say that?

This property, she moved to New York from this?

I will explain later.

Taking Kevin's hint I cease from asking any further questions.

Beth up for a brief stroll?

Sure

Charles could you pull over, Beth and I will walk the rest of the way.

Pulling over Kevin with all that is going on, Thomas and Donaldson will discreetly be with you.

Sure *Getting out of the SUV Kevin and I begin our stroll.*

A stroll Mr. Walker?

I wanted to show you where I spent my summers and often school breaks.

Here?

Yes. See Mrs. Clarke was fired by Blanche immediately after my first visit to their home.

Why?

Blanche found out Mrs. Clarke told me about my father. From what I learned years later Blanche basically had a breakdown after my father was killed. She banned any of the staff to speak of him. She restricted grandfather from talking about him, not mentioning his name even. But when grandfather found out Blanche fired Mrs. Clarke after working for them since before my father's birth grandfather purchased this property shortly after and asked Mrs.

Clarke to live here and managed the property. A few years ago he signed the property over to her.

Wow that was very generous of him.

Yes but well deserved. Other than Adele she was the other mother figure. Mrs. Clarke took care of me consistently since the age of ten and not once during that time did she say one negative word about Blanche. In fact she would drill into my head Blanche's loss of my father took a toll on her and was having a difficult time coping. But I have to say Adele was ecstatic, relieved even that I didn't stay at grandfather's home that I wasn't around Blanche.

But Mrs. Clarke gave all this up to move to New York with us?

I'm – we are the closest thing to family.

Laughing Do I see cows?

Yes at least four different breed of cattle.

Don't tell me, you worked here on the farm?

Smiling, I worked her on the ranch.

You say I surprise you, you're blowing me away with this info *and I laugh.*

Come on, *laughing* if you're not hungry I know my son or daughter is. Let's head to the house.

Entering a real live South Fork home, Kevin leads us to the back patio where we find Mrs. Clarke and Charles sitting.

Kevin how's your grandfather?

He seems okay. Our visit was cut short a bit. Blanche came to visit.

Sighing, Are you okay?

No worries Mrs. Clarke

Looking over to Charles So she knows about Beth and the baby?

Yes Mrs. Clarke we had a brief encounter. *Mrs. Clarke presenting concerned* Why? Something wrong?

No Beth, I…. Beth – Kevin just be careful of her *again making eye contact with Charles.*

Mrs. Clarke please don't worry k*issing her on the cheek* I'm going to take Beth up and get settled in.

Smiling now Kevin you can take the master

No my old room is just fine as long as it is okay with you.

Certainly it is. While you two are getting settled in I will prepare brunch. Beth any request?

Whatever you prepare both me and this *pointing to my stomach* little person will enjoy.

Walking through the house the comfort of home sets in. Photographs of Kevin everywhere. Walking up the stairs pictures of Kevin with his grandfather, with John and Adele and at the top of the stair a beautiful picture of a young Mrs. Clarke with a very young picture of Kevin. Both with very large smiles. Entering Kevin's room a smile emerges immediately. I look over to Kevin and I see by the twinkle in his eyes he is home.

So now I have to pray that our child not only has your looks but your intelligence as well *pointing to a wall of academic achievements.*

Sporting a cheesy smile well what can I say?

What did Adele do, send all your awards here?

Not exactly, whatever happened in Alabama and NY Adele made sure Mrs. Clarke and Grandfather knew about it, hence making copies of awards, newspaper clippings etc.

Newspaper clippings?

Kevin points to a bulletin board hanging on the corner wall. I played a little ball, was on the football, baseball and basketball teams.

So wait you were a tri – athlete, a triple threat?

I was!

Huh….

Pulling me close to him what do you mean by huh?

I just realized the probability of you actually having the stamina to jump my bones in our eighties is quite possible.

Laughing told you one way or another I will…

As Kevin and I continue to discuss his achievements we are interrupted by Charles.

Excuse me Beth but Kevin we need to talk.

Charles did anything happen back home?

No Beth, just planning the afternoon

Ok…. *But I know it is more than planning based on the eye exchange between Kevin and Charles.*

Baby will you be ok up here?

Right now Kevin I am in heaven. I get to peek into your childhood. I will be just fine. But I also plan to go down and help Mrs. Clarke.

Maybe a nap?

Nah don't worry I am fine.

Kevin and Charles leave and I continue to scan the many pictures and awards displayed throughout Kevin's childhood room. I hope you *(rubbing my stomach)* inherit your dad's genes. *Looking now at the pictures displayed on his dresser I do a double take. A picture of a beautiful woman embracing a very handsome Kevin look alike. In this moment I realize I am looking at Kevin's parents, looking very in love. My heart immediately feels heavy. I take the picture in hand and sit on the edge of the bed. Kevin is the spitting image of his father with his mother's beautiful light eyes. So engrossed in thought I don't realize Kevin is standing in the doorway.*

Mrs. Clarke held on to that picture after my father died and gave it to me for my High School graduation gift.

Kevin your mother was beautiful. You have her eyes and your dad, it is you…

I was blessed with two beautiful parents.

Yes you were. Kevin you do know I would be fine with naming our baby after your mom or dad.

Walking and sitting next to me Baby I will leave that up to you ….. But thank you for considering. Besides I thought you were going to name our son after your dad.

I've considered but I wouldn't make a decision like that by myself. Now what is going on? You've had an annoyed look since coming back.

Nothing to worry about.

Kevin what is it?

……………

Kevin!

Blanche is trying to have grandfather discharged to her home.

What?

Beth she's not happy that I'm here, she barely knew about you and the baby….. In her head you're the enemy. I made a big mistake bringing you here.

Kevin what does JD want?

I don't know. Since leaving Blanche has remained by JD's side

A good thing isn't it?

Beth you don't understand, she and JD live very separate lives. She - her wanting JD home is not without motive.

Well let's go down and eat then head out.

Beth wait…..

Kevin?

I would like you to stay here.

Huh?

I'm going to go back with Charles and you… I would like you to stay back with Mrs. Clarke.

Kevin, I'm from New York... Queens at that. I can handle my own... I'm going with you or without you.

Exhaling Beth real rough and tough neighborhood! Queens Village – Bellrose... Real tough neighborhood.... *We both laugh* Alright but Beth we will leave immediately if she starts anything.

Arriving back to the hospital, the media circus from earlier seems to have dissipated a bit. I can only assume confirmation of JD's stability decreases the need to know more at this time. Making our way to JD's room an uneasy feeling kicks in. I internally calm myself but based on the hold Kevin has on my hand he too is feeling uneasy about this visit.

Hi JD, how are you feeling?

I'm feeling and doing much better

Grandfather you look better.....

Thank you Kevin. Having both of you here helps but Beth please sit. How are you feeling?

JD we are doing fine.

Listen, I don't want you and Kevin worrying about me. I'm fine! Kevin did you and Charles talk?

Yes grandfather we did. You and I can discuss the matter when you're feeling stronger.

Why do I get the feeling Kevin didn't review everything with me?

Son I don't mean to pressure you but decisions need to be made now. I only trust two people with my company and that would be you and Charles.

Now I know Kevin didn't tell me everything

Grandfather you and I will talk tomorrow about this, until then how should we plan for your recovery?

Hopefully I will be discharged tomorrow. Beth did you get settled in? Where are you two staying?

At the ranch. Mrs. Clarke flew in with us.

The mention of Mrs. Clarke's name sparks a bit of energy into JD. By his response one would think a bit of romance happened or happening... But the thought of JD and Mrs. Clarke makes me think of my being called a whore.

Grandfather are you returning home or should I have Mrs. Clarke prepare the ranch?

Sighing deeply Kevin I think I need to be home with Blanche.

Then Charles will setup a security team to remain with you.

Kevin that is completely unnecessary.

Interrupting Grandfather if you want me to consider your request then you must agree to have a detail with you at all times.

But Blanche will not agree to this.

Grandfather.... The only way.

Forcing a smile enough about me *just then JD's cardiologist enters*

Mr. Durand how are you feeling?

Much better and ready to go home.

Turning to Kevin and me you must be Kevin?

Yes, *extending his hand to Dr. Katz to shake* and my wife Beth

Your grandfather speaks fondly of both of you.

Could you please summarize what caused the heart attack and his care from this moment on?

Luckily your grandfather arrived here when he did. We were able to intervene early, performing an Angioplasty which went well, a standard procedure. We were able to unblock the artery by inserting a stint. Now it is up to Mr. Durand to follow his diet and take better care of himself.

Oh he will I assure you. *JD looking amused by my statement.*

When can he be discharged?

If your grandfather continues to do well and no complications tomorrow afternoon the earliest.

Care at home?

Rest for the next week. Taking it easy. *Looking over to JD* but we have to get control of your sugar.

I know - I know!

Also no more sixteen to twenty hour work days and traveling across the map as often as you do.

Dr. Katz now you're being unreasonable.

Grandfather doesn't sound like you have too much of choice.

Kevin I'm fine!

Well it was nice meeting you two. Mr. Durand I will see you in the morning.

Thank you Dr. Katz

As Dr. Katz exits Charles enters with an uneasy look Kevin can I speak with you?

Not answering Kevin walks out into the hallway. I resume my seat next to JD from earlier today.

JD you know you're more than welcomed to stay with Kevin and me. Actually I would love it if you came home with us.

Beth thank you for offering but I can't. My place is here with Blanche and I'm truly sorry for this morning.

You don't need to apologize to me, besides it isn't everyday I'm mistaken for whore.... I thought I was looking sort of dowdy lately but Blanche's take of me gave me a glimmer of hope. *We both laugh*

Beth you have a smile that lights up a room.

Thank you... But don't try and sweet talk me mister, sugar levels are high?

Guess my snacking has been a bit out of control.

A bit huh?

Just a smidgen

JD *presenting more serious* should I be concerned about you going home?

Taking my hand Beth I will be ok. Blanche, was the love of my life. When Jackson died a piece of her died with him. The woman you met yesterday *sighing* Blanche hasn't gotten over Jackson's passing.

And she blames Kevin's mother?

Externally she does but internally I know she blames herself.

For the next week promise me you will stay in contact with me?

Seeing the worried look on my face oh sweet Beth I will but I don't want you worrying about me. I need you to take care of yourself.

Smiling the pictures of you and Kevin at Mrs. Clarke's home warms my heart and until this morning I didn't know what your son looked like.

You saw the picture of Jackson and Amanda?

Yes....your grandson has his father's handsome looks and his mother's beautiful eyes.

Opening his wallet On my worst days these pictures get me through. My beautiful wife on our wedding day over 50 years ago, my son only a few days old, my grandson and me on our first fishing trip, my grandson and his beautiful wife on their wedding day and this one, my son looking his happiest.

You have a copy of the picture of your son and Amanda...... JD! But how did you get a picture from our wedding day?

From Adele.

As JD and I continue to reminisce Charles and Kevin returns.

Kevin everything ok?

Yes but Beth we need to get going *said with a look of uneasiness*

Kevin?

Grandfather I don't want another encounter as this morning. Blanche is on her way up and we are going to head out.

Kissing JD remember daily contact sir.

I will Beth

Alright I love you and hopefully will see you soon.

I love you too Beth

Grandfather Charles and I will meet you here in the morning.

Great. You get Beth back to Mrs. Clarke's for some rest. Beth take care of my great – grandchild.

Oh I will...... *Leaving JD in this moment Kevin's presents again with a look of worry. But along with worry I see the true love he has for JD.*

Mrs. Clarke this is the best BBQ ever.

Beth I've never seen you eat so much in one sitting.

I think it's this Texas air. I'm a bit sad that we have to go back so soon.

Really?

Yes...... why Kevin?

I can head back and you and Mrs. Clarke could stay for a bit.

Kevin!

Beth not a bad idea.

Charles not happening

Beth we can stay a few more days.

Mrs. Clarke thank you, I would love to but I need to tie up the last few matters with the community center. November 1st will be here in a flash. By the way *turning to Kevin* did you find anything out about Michael?

Exchanging eye contact with Charles no not yet. Mrs. Clarke are the old paddle boats down by the lake?

They are

Beth up for a moonlight boat ride?

Yes I am *but don't think I'm not aware of you changing the subject!*

Beth I'll leave a plate in the warming draw for you.

Somewhat embarrassed Thank you. Alright Mr. Walker, lead the way.

With my hand in his, Kevin leads the way. Beth are you really up to this?

I am... Kevin what's troubling you?

Here let's sit for a moment *Taking seat in the grass under the moonlight which bounces off the water. Exhaling deeply* Beth grandfather would like me to run the company.

I had a suspicion this matter came up. Have you made a decision?

I wouldn't decide on something like this without talking it out with you first.

I appreciate that Kevin but this is a decision only you can make. All I ask is that the man who sits with me this very moment will be that same man, a loving and caring husband and damn good father, a father I know you will be.

Kissing my hand you and my child *smiling* possibly children will always be my priority.

Ignoring the more than one possibility Then why the hesitance?

Beth exposing you, my family to the world. I can take care of myself but you and the baby? I can barely protect the two of you right now.

Kevin I will support any decision you make but why now?

From what Charles informed me of, JD wants to step down but I think it has more to do with Blanche which is something else we will need to deal with.

I don't follow Kevin.

I'm sure Blanche is concerned with grandfathers will, who he will leave the company to. Although I've told him of my non interest he continues to present the possibility.

What if you choose not to accept?

He will break the company up and sell it off.

How do you feel about that?

Before you, before us I would have immediately said no and actually volunteered to help sell it but since you and now us I find myself wanting more not only for myself but for us.

Kevin I don't want you to decide to do this for financial gain. We - you, me and this little person here would do just fine on the two incomes we have. The house and cars do not make who we are. We can do without.

I know we can. A lot to consider. But right this moment *looking around* I would like to make love to you under this beautiful late summer Texas sky.

Kevin sure we won't be trampled on by cows?

Laughing Beth this isn't the pasture.

Then in that case I'm all yours as always.

Chapter Seventeen: Back to Business

Rochelle I can't believe we are officially up and running.

Believe it Beth and the feedback from the Mayor's office has been outstanding. From what I've been told any and all grants we apply for will be approved.

Wow.... But why?

Look around you. JD basically started a revitalization here. Opening the center in an area where foreclosed buildings and homes are the highest in the New York City area. Needless to say the show of support that came out for the ribbon cutting. Multi-millionaires, billionaires even and since, the inquiries regarding property availability and incentives have been amazing. JD started something here.

Well we better make sure we live up to everyone's expectations which brings me to the mobile clinic. Were you able to look at the proposal?

Yes I have. On paper sounds great but the concern would be local hospitals willingness to work with us. Will our team assessments and recommendations be enough for admittance and at least a 72 hour hold for mental health concerns? More importantly holding someone until proper placement could be made if extended placement is needed?

Same questions I have. I set up meetings with all four hospitals. Carla included the dates onto your calendar. But I think the sale pitch is our ability to access from the field which will decrease their issues of over populated emergency rooms and the ridiculous wait times of four to five hours to be seen. This will be a first for this area of Brooklyn where health care is not a priority.

I agree. Okay what else is on the agenda?

Smiling the Holidays

Beth no… No No No….

Oh come on….. Aren't you a wee bit excited? For the first time in eight years we aren't out begging and pleading for donations. Going into our own pockets to insure everyone has food and gifts for both Thanksgiving and Christmas?

Beth…

This is the first year we can give a gift basket to everyone and not by lottery.

Okay Beth…….

Excuse me Beth but you have a call on Line two.

Thanks Carla

I'm taking this opportunity to leave. Thinking about the Holidays Beth? Year after year you begin to celebrate earlier and earlier. For the past eight years, since meeting you Mrs. Walker I think I've engaged in the celebration of Christmas more than Hanukah. My parents would not be proud.

Laughing Hey reminder I learned and performed the "Dreidel" song for your family how many times? What started as a bet turned into an annual event!

Which reminds me, you're on at 7:30 p.m. this year…. *Laughing* and this year not at my home but my Synagogue.

No longer laughing Rochelle your joking right? *Exiting my office laughing* Rochelle not funny.

Beth that caller is still on hold

Okay picking up now Carla…. Beth Walker

Beth please don't hang up.

Michael?

Yes… Beth I was hoping you and I could meet?

Michael I can't. What do you want?

I would rather talk to you in person, please?

Michael?

I'm about a block away. Can I come by? I really need to speak with you.

Michael we will not be alone

I understand. I'll be by in about ten minutes.

Hanging up with Michael I call Kevin. No answer. I won't leave a message, it will just worry him. I'll review with Thomas and Donaldson. Heading to the security office that of course JD and Kevin made sure was in place along with the high tech surveillance system

Hey.....

Mrs. Walker everything okay?

Yes but I'm meeting Michael in a few minutes here.

Mrs. Walker is Mr. Walker aware of your plan?

No Thomas. I called but he didn't pick up.

Taking out his cell phone Mrs. Walker I will call Mr. Walker and let him know.

That is not necessary, I would like one of you to be with me. Nothing more needs to be said or done.

Mr. Walker will have a problem with this plan.

Thomas I will handle Mr. Walker. Donaldson are you available?

Sure Mrs. Walker *I guess he senses my anger building. I know Thomas is only doing his job but damn!*

Thanks, I'll meet you in the small conference room.

By the time I make it back to my office, Carla announces Michael's arrival. Carla please escort him to the small conference room. I'll be in in a minute.

Entering the conference room Donaldson suggest by way of pointing for me to sit in a chair near the door. He stands by my side and Thomas who too is in the room stands behind Michael.

Beth thank you for seeing me.

Michael what do you want?

Beth I came to apologize. I didn't mean what I said.

Michael you need to get your life together, you need help.

Beth that's why I'm here. I need your help.

What?

Beth I want help with my drinking and I didn't know where to start.

Knock….. Knock……..

Come in…

I should not be surprised to see Kevin entering the room. I wouldn't expect anything less from fucking Thomas…. He called Kevin!

Beth can I speak with you….. Now! *Anger written across his face*

Excuse me Michael, I'll be back in a moment.

Following Kevin into my office I prepare myself for the fallout.

Beth what the hell are you doing?

He called and asked if he could meet with me. I tried to call you but I got your voice mail.

And you couldn't leave a message? You couldn't tell him no until you and I talked?

Kevin come on…

Beth are you fucking kidding me? Get a damn clue. Your eight months pregnant and your meeting with an asshole that physically assaulted you not even a good three months ago?

Kevin….

Beth what the fuck does he want?

He says he needs help.

What type of help?

I don't know you interrupted!

Not amused Beth!

Kevin whatever, I'm not going to argue with you over Michael, just not! Will you be returning to the conference room with me?

Not answering, Kevin leaves my office and enters the conference room. I follow in tow. I retake my seat and Kevin stands behind me.

Michael what do you want?

Looking at Kevin rather than me I was hoping you could help me get into a program.

What type of program?

For my drinking

Why here and not North Carolina?

Because I'm here now.

Before I can give a response Kevin chimes in I will gladly assist you but Beth will not.

Turning to look at Kevin his expression prompts me to withhold any comments.

I'm not here to cause any problems but I would like Beth's assistance.

Will not happen *Kevin's tone presenting even more agitated.*

Michael if you really want the help it shouldn't matter who provides the information.

Staring intensely at Kevin Beth I apologize for anything I may have said or did but I will get help elsewhere.

Then good luck to you Michael.

Opening the door for Michael Kevin motions to Donaldson and Thomas to walk Michael out. Closing the door behind them Kevin motions for me to remain seated.

What is it Kevin?

You're pissed, oh well…. If he calls I'm to be contacted immediately. If he returns Thomas and Donaldson will handle it. No more contact. Am I making myself clear?

First of all I'm a grown ass woman. I do not appreciate being talked down to as if I'm a child. Secondly my father is six feet under the last time I checked and your claim to fatherhood will make his or her debut in a month.

Beth I'm not going to play this game with you. I'm done here.

Whatever Kevin. I need to get back to work.

Not saying a word Kevin exit's the conference room, slamming the door behind himself. I begin debating with myself if I was wrong, if Kevin was correct with not allowing me to assist Michael directly. As my inner debate continues a knock at the door.

Come in

Beth a Ms. Black is here to see you

Oh please, show her in

Ms. Black how are you?

Standing to greet and hug Ms. Black, Ms. Black is taken by surprise by the sight of my very large belly.

Mrs. Walker hello to both of you. When are you due?

In about a month.

Wow congratulations.

Thank you. What brings you by?

I had a doctor's appointment nearby and just wanted to say hello.

Your appointment went well?

Yes. But wow look at this place. I saw the ribbon cutting on the news but TV doesn't do justice to this place appearance.

We were blessed with a great benefactor.
How are the kids?

Everyone is fine. I have to get going. I just wanted to say hello.

I'm glad you did. Stop by again soon.

I will.

Sitting back at my desk I debate if I should call Kevin and apologize. For every reason I think I should, I have twice the reason not to. I'll just address the issue tonight when I get home, which looking at my watch is already five-thirty. Packing up my bag Donaldson already at my door.

Ready to go Mrs. Walker?

I am… *Taking my briefcase from me Donaldson leads the way.*

Carla Dr. Harris has an evening group tonight. Can you please remind him to lockup and set the alarm?

Actually his assistant couldn't stay and I said I would cover. I'll lockup myself.

Okay, great. Have a great evening

Arriving home approximately around seven I'm surprised Kevin isn't home yet.

Hi Mrs. Clarke, Kevin didn't arrive home yet?

Hi Beth, no he called and said he would be working late.

Oh *really Kevin? You couldn't call me and let me know?*

Beth I have dinner waiting.

Actually Mrs. Clarke I'm going to go up and Change I'll eat a bit later. You go on I will be fine.

Okay Beth, good night.

Good night Mrs. Clarke *Making my way upstairs I immediately take off my clothes and run a bath. After about a thirty minute soak I lay across my bed flicking through the channels to find something to watch. However the television must have been watching me, I drift into a comfortable slumber.*

Around four in the morning I am awakened by my little attachment movements. Turning over to look into my husband's handsome face I am startled by his side of the bed being untouched. I immediately get up and look in the nursery, no Kevin. I go downstairs and look through out, still no Kevin. Beginning to panic I return to my bedroom and pull out my cell for any possible messages. Inhaling deeply two missed calls with two voice messages both from Kevin. First Beth I won't be home till late. *Second* Still here in Brooklyn. Probably won't be home until the morning. *Both messages Kevin's voice presents with the same tone from earlier. No apology, no sincerity and no I love you. Does this son of the bitch think he is punishing me? Really Kevin. Not giving any further thought I attempt to go back to sleep but I can't. I lay awake until six and decide to get up, dress and leave before Kevin gets home. Not wanting to bother*

Donaldson I decide to drive myself in. About to leave I leave a note for Donaldson on the message board. But just as I tact my note to the board I find a note from Mrs. Clarke stating JD will be in New York today and will stop by the center. A smile immediately emerges upon my face. I leave my note for Donaldson and begin my way into work.

Chapter Eighteen: The Way You Got Him is the Way You Lose Him

Arriving to the office around seven thirty I am immediately startled by Donaldson and Thomas standing right behind me.

Good Morning Mrs. Walker

Ah Good Morning?

Did you forget about your security detail? *Thomas says with complete sarcasm. I turn to Donaldson who usually tries to be a buffer between Thomas and me but this morning only a look of anger.*

Continuing to look at Donaldson I decided to come in early and did not want to bother either of you.

Mrs. Walker our job is to be bothered. *Taking out his cellphone.* Mr. Walker we all are here at the center……. Thank you sir.

Beth do not lose it on this man… Don't! Really? Every move I make….. Whatever.

Refusing to acknowledge either any longer I head to my office and wait until both Thomas and Donaldson make their way to the security office. Once the coast is clear I begin to prepare the conference room for our first parenting group being held at the center. By the time I'm done the center is filled with both employees and patrons. Looking around I am overcome with joy, to see a dream come together as it has. In this moment I think of my husband who with JD made this happen. Although still pissed, I smile at the thought of my husband holding me in his arms and caressing me gently from the top of my head, ending at my bottom. But my midmorning beginning erotic thought is interrupted.

Beth you have a call on line three

Thanks Carla...... Beth Walker

Good Morning Mrs. Walker my name is Anthony Anderson with St. Angus Rehabilitation Center.

How can I help you?

Your husband asked that I call and inform you of his admittance.

Admittance? My husband doesn't require such a program.

Mrs. Walker this may be difficult to hear but sometimes family has a tendency to be oblivious to the addiction. But I'm sure with counseling for you and your husband we can work through many of the signs that are frankly right in front of you.

This has to be some type of joke. Ah Mr. Anderson, I need to put you on hold

Sure.

This doesn't make any sense. I'll call Kevin. Calling his cell phone I get his voice mail. I'll see what Donaldson and Thomas knows. Dialing the security office Hi Thomas could you and Donaldson come to my office?

On our way Mrs. Walker *Less than 30 seconds both enter.*

Have either of you spoke with Kevin in the past hour?

No, is there a problem?

I don't know Donaldson, I have a Mr. Anderson on hold. He says Kevin is in rehab???? Could he be undercover especially since he didn't come home last night?

Thomas and Donaldson exchange a look

Something you two want to share?

Mrs. Walker are you sure the gentleman is not referring to Mr. Morris?

He said my husband. Shit he better not have *answering the line and putting it on speaker* Hello Mr. Anderson?

Yes

I apologize for putting you on hold for so long but I need to confirm, are you calling on behalf of Michael Morris?

Yes Mrs. Walker, your husband!

No Mr. Morris and I have been divorced for over ten years.

Oh, I would assume then the two of you have a cordial relationship? He has indicted you as point of contact.

No I'm sorry it should not be me.

Mrs. Walker I understand there may have been some difficulties in the past but I don't think it would be beneficial to Michael at this time to avoid communication. This is a crucial time for him.

Mr. Anderson I'm sorry I cannot.

Could I put Mr. Morris on, he is here in my office.

Wait he has been sitting with you throughout this conversation?

Yes can I put him on with you?

No you may not.

Mrs. Walker I don't think you understand from a clinical perspective the detriment of this type of rejection could do.

Excuse Mr. Anderson, your calling me at my place of work where I am the Co-Executive Director. I 'm a certified licensed Social worker who is also CASAC Certified. Do not try to insinuate any harm I could do in regards to Mr. Morris's rehabilitation.

Interrupting me Then I would expect you better than anyone else to understand the need for communication.

Seeing my frustration increasing Donaldson replies Excuse me, Mrs. Walker has confirmed she will not engage in any communications with Mr. Morris. Please do not call Mrs. Walker here again. *And Donaldson hangs up.*

Thank you!

No problem Mrs. Walker. If he calls again please let us know immediately.

I will.

As the day continues I can't help to wonder why Michael would give out my name and number in general but as his point of contact. Is he trying to push Kevin's buttons? Speaking of Kevin not one call. He's taking this a bit too far. Based on Thomas's call this morning he must care. A smile emerges. I will be the bigger person and apologize.

Knock…. Knock….

Come in

Beth Ms. Black is one line one. She sounds very upset.

Okay, thank you. And you don't need to stay behind. It is already after five. I will lock up.

Thanks Beth and good night.

Hello Ms. Black its Beth, everything okay?

……. No Beth

Ms. Black what's wrong?

Barely able to speak through her sobbing Could I come by and talk to you?

Mrs. Black I can easily come to you.

I'm actually nearby, please! *And the sobbing increases*

I will be here waiting. See you soon.

I guess no better time to call Kevin. Hey baby I'm going to be a bit late this evening. Angela Black just called and asked if she could meet me. Doesn't sound as if things are going well for her. I'll call you when I'm on the road and yes I will make Thomas and Donaldson aware. But I don't want this to be awkward for Ms. Black. I want to give her as much privacy as I can so I will ask Thomas and Donaldson to stay back. Okay I Love you and I missed you last night.

Keeping my word I walk to the security office to speak with Thomas and Donaldson Hey I'm going to be late this evening. I have someone coming in who is in crisis. I need to give her my full attention and privacy. We will be meeting in my office. When I'm done I will let you know. *Turning to Thomas* And I already informed Kevin. *With a forced smile I exit the security office. Walking back to my office I see Ms. Black in the waiting area.*

Beth thank you for seeing me I didn't know who else to call.

Ms. Black what's wrong?

Everything, I feel like I'm losing control.

Come follow me *leading the way to my office* have a seat.

Mrs. Walker have you ever had a day where you felt your life was over? Done with?

Ms. Black - Angela what is it? Are the children ok?

The children are fine. It is me.... It is always me.

Sensing there is a reason she is wearing sunglasses at dusk Angela please take off your sun glasses.

Weeping I can't

Please

Removing her glasses my heart sinks Angela what happened?

....

Her slow movement to reposition herself in the chair suggest further harm has been done. Angela where else are you hurt?

....

Angela I'm going to lift your shirt *raising her shirt to her shoulders unveils her recent beating. So recent her skin hasn't begun to heal.* Angela who did this to you?

....

Angela I'm going to call for an ambulance and you and I will go to the hospital together.

No hospital

Angela you can barely move. You need medical attention.

I can't go... Mrs. Walker sorry to waste your time. I need to go home.

Angela the person that did this to you should be arrested and charged.

....

Angela?

Weeping Mrs. Walker I.... No. He didn't mean to do this.

Where are the kids?

With my mother.

Does your mother know about this? Did she see what I see?

Shaking her head No, they were already at her home.

Tell me what happened.

He has been coming by more and more lately. I thought he was trying to make it work, to have a family. But once again he made a fool out of me.

How?

By putting me and the kids last, not making us his main focus.

What led to this?

We planned to be alone for a few days to talk out how we could make our relationship work. But he arrived drunk and the rest is history.

Where is he now?

Why?

For your safety!

There's only one thing that can insure my safety!

And what would that be?

In this moment Mrs. Black's demeanor completely changes. Her voice and body movement presents threating. No longer seeming as the fragile woman needing help but rather a woman with a plan. You finally getting the fuck out of our lives?

Taken back by Angela's comment Me?

Laughing with tears streaming down her face Oh yes you. *Rising to her feet, Angela stands and hovers over me. Fear begins to sets in.*

Angela what have I done?

Your mere presence.

Attempting to stand to my feet I am shoved back down. Angela's demeanor goes from a woman with barely any strength to this threatening intimidating woman standing right in front of me, right this moment. It's as if I triggered this emotion but how? What I said? But what did I say? What the hell did I say or do? Angela please?

Please what? Do you know you are one winning bitch?

Bitch? Excuse me.... *Anger building within me*
That's right Bitch!

Attempting to get up once more I am slapped across the face. Keep your ass down. I want you to be comfortable for our game. You like playing games don't you? Come on we played before. But this time it will be all about Elizabeth Morris now Walker.

She can't be, no what the fuck.... All this time it was you? Why?

Because you are you. Do you know I was actually beginning to like you? Then you get married? Happiness…. Now a fucking baby... You don't deserve happiness. You make me sick!

Realization sets in. The bruises today and from the past done by the hand of Michael. Michael did this to you. Why?

With a large smile Why? Because he's a broken man, the man you made him to be!

What are you talking about? Why did he do this to you?

Because of you. It is always you. He came to you for help and you turned him away. He reached out for help and you spit on him.

He told you this?

Why wouldn't he. We love each other. His pain is my pain and the cause of the pain is you! Do you know how many times he has told me you took everything he had, leaving him with nothing? How you still call him for support, trying to fuck him? Is that baby really that sweet detective Walker's?

Angela what you heard is far from the truth. *Pushing my way up from my seat I'm hit once again across the face with a closed fist.*

Move again and I will blow your fucking brains out... Do you understand? *A gun pointing directly at my stomach.*

Please don't do this.

Oh we are doing this and unlike last time I will succeed.

Angela please let me go. Kevin is expecting me and he will be coming to look for me.

That's Wonderful.....He will find you, just not alive.

Her words hit me from within. I begin to shake. Angela please don't do this, please. My baby... I don't want my baby's life to end before having a chance to live. Please.

Like you gave that poor unborn baby? Oh right you killed it. *Smiling with tears falling* As much as I want to spare each of your lives I can't. Sorry!

But why? Is Michael behind all of this?

Michael *trying to hold back from crying* is a broken man thanks to you! I don't know how Karen put up with him. But she turned out to be a weak woman anyway!

Did you killed her?

Smiling Wasn't my initial goal but she… she turned against Michael.

Trying to hold back my tears She turned against Michael?

She refused to allow Michael to see his children. Provide for them.

Michael is the father of your children?

Yes and she couldn't deal with that. The more pressure she put on Michael the more depressed he became.

And expressing his frustration by way of physically assaulting you is okay?

Because of you he doesn't know no other way.

And I'm the reason Michal abused you? Turned his back on his children. Me?

Are you really asking me? Look at me, my children how we live. We have nothing and you living high on life

Angela you have it all wrong.

No I have it right. When was the last time you went without a meal? Slept in your car? Depending on welfare and food stamps to live. Tell me, when was the last time!

Angela... No I've never received any type of assistance. But I struggled every day of my life to pull myself up.

Well fucking good for you. Hard to do when you have fucking four children and doing it all on your own.

Angela I'm sorry.

Tears trickling down her face you should be. You caused a lot of heartache and now it is time for you to pay up.

Angela I don't understand. I've only treated you with kindness.

After the birth of my second child Michael completely dismissed me. Letting me know I was a fucking easy lay and had no intention to support me or my children. "I have a family already and don't want or need another". To bring his point home, during a drunken rage he broke three of my ribs and broke my nose.

My revenge *laughing* I called his wife and told her everything. Karen didn't fight me but instead showed up to my door two days later with clothes for my boys and food. She never once asked me to prove anything, she just knew. Month after month a check was mailed to me. She called often and made sure my boys had gifts during the holidays. We became friends then lovers, yes lovers that's how I found out about you..... The root of all Michael's problems. Michael had no clue about Karen and my relationship and while with Karen I didn't need him, Karen filled this void *(pointing to her heart).* She treated me with respect, knew what needed to be said and did what was needed to be done. She loved me. I didn't hear from Michael for over two years. Then out of the blue he showed up at my door once again, sorry for everything. Yes we fucked and I became pregnant again. He promised to be there for me and he kept his promise for a little while, until his daughter died! Long story short Karen found out and the bitch went cuckoo. She invited me to North Carolina and while fucking me the bitch reveled what she knew about me and Michael and attempted to kill me. But based on who is standing here now talking, we know who lost the battle.

Angela you killed her in self-defense, you can explain that to the authorities. Don't make trouble for yourself....please let me go.

No I have to finish what I started if not for me then for Karen.

For Karen? You just said she tried to take your life. Why are you seeking vengeance on her behalf?

Yelling You just don't get it do you? DO YOU? You're the root of all our hurt. You're the cancer. You made us who we are. You made Michael who he is. The blood I shed is all due to you.

Angela I'm sorry

You don't mean it.

Your right I don't! I will say and do anything to save my baby. Is this honest enough?

Smiling is the real Beth coming through? But too late.

Calmer voice Angela how am I to blame? If nothing more please just help me understand.

Look at me!

....

This is your handy work. Do you know how it feels to be hit, taunted and humiliated? Do you know how it feels to be called a bitch and beat in front of your children?

Yes I do. I've been through everything you have and maybe more. I endured the same abuse. I on many days went without food. I was sixteen weeks pregnant and was beat severely. I prayed often, asking God to take my child before birth. I know very well. To get rid of my misery I tried to kill myself after my final brutal ass kicking *removing my watch and bangle to expose my self-inflicted wounds.* I did this to myself, me.... I did this to me. I claim all responsibility. I don't blame Michael, it was a decision I made. But what hurts the most, the man Michael was supposed to be, showed me how much of a low life he was – he is. That low life fuck told the police he came home and found me like that, with bruises and all. Now how fucked up is that?

Presenting with a softer expression But you could have put an end to it!

Me? Possibly but I was young and Naive. I was embarrassed and where was I going to go? Back home? In my head back then, going home wasn't an option. The only way out of it I thought was taking my own life. I didn't know better. I didn't want to know better.

What about Karen, you got involved with him knowing he was already in a relationship. Knowing he had a child.

Wait.... I've always been a believer of "The way you got him is the way you lose him". I would have never engage in a relationship with someone already involved.

. . . .

The same man you claim as your man is the low life I had, a sick fucking bastard, a user who will drain you emotionally and give nothing in return.

But Karen believed you took him from her.

Never! Michael was a nasty sick son of a bitch way before I met him. We fall for the charm and his professed love. But slowly and surely the monster comes to the surface.

"The way you got him is the way you lose him". I did that didn't I?

Initially you didn't know about Karen

But I knew at some point!

Yes.....

Beth I'm.....

That doesn't matter now. What matters is your wellbeing. Take charge of you.

Beth I...

Interrupted by my cell rings..... I should answer it No!

Now the office line rings I should answer....

(((I said no)))! Get up.....

Just then I hear JD's voice Beth honey, everything okay? Beth?

Whispering Who is that?

My grandfather in law. Please don't harm him.

Knocking on my office door, not waiting for a response JD opens the door and walks in Beth I've been calling you.

With tears falling I mouth "I'm sorry". *JD presenting strong realizes what he walked in on. Angela continues pointing the gun directly at my stomach demands that JD takes a seat.*

What is going on here?

Awe granddaddy cares? Lucky lucky you Elizabeth, another person who fucking loves and

295

cares about you. But does he love you enough to take a bullet for you?

I will do anything to spare her life.

Awe how sweet.... But you look familiar.

I will give you anything you want just let Beth go, I will remain.

Your Jackson Durnad... No fucking way. *And in this moment the anger in Angela's voice increases.* It never fucking ends for you does it.

Let Beth go. I will stay and you have my word anything you want I will make sure you have.

Jackson Durand...... Sorry money can't buy everything and certainly not today.

Angela please just let us go.

Look don't fucking ask me again. Beth stand up..... Stand the fuck up now.

Crying and trying to raise to a standing position as fast as I can please don't do this please.

With the gun still pointed at my stomach you ever had one of those days where you look forward to doing something you've wanted to do for a long time? *Smiling* that's how I feel. I've waited too long for this day and it's finally here.

Then let my grandfather go. He was never a part of your plan.

But he is now so.... Sorry.

Angela for your children, your sweet babies don't do this.

Looking at my wrist Death is the only way for peace isn't it?

No making peace with self gives peace.

Crying Do you know how many times I prayed for peace not for me but my children? Do you remember the first time we met? I do….. You put a smile on my son's face. He hadn't done that in a long time. You didn't pass judgment, you didn't ask any questions. I actually felt good for a few days. Then it happened again, stupid me I let him in. Back to the name calling back to the fighting. *Sighing deeply,* Every morning I promise myself for my children I cried my last tears yesterday, just like the song says. *Smiling* but by the time I close my eyes to go to bed, I've already cried a river. I find myself asking God why he would let me go through this. I'm still waiting for an answer, a sign…. Just something. But all I get is the same from the day before, it never ends. I know Karen is at peace now. Mr. Durand you can go.

Not without Beth.

JD go… It will be okay *Tears fall faster* Just tell Kevin I'm sorry and he will always always be my all, my everything. Tell him it wasn't until him that I knew what love is, what happiness feels like…… *Smiling* Just tell him that please.

I'm not leaving you Beth

Yes you are, go now!

Mr. Durand - Beth open the door

Walking to the door I hear the barrel of the gun clicking, being prepared to be fired. Turning the knob I pray Heavenly father just allow my baby to live please. Take care of my sister and help Kevin through this, please. Daddy I need your hand now, guide me home….. *I open the door and step to the side for JD to exit.*

Beth look at me *I turn to the barrel of the gun being pointed directly at me, I close my eyes. I feel a tight pain in my chest and I can't breathe. I hear Kevin's voice and feel his touch but it fades. I open my eyes and there he is as promised, my father with his hand extended waiting for me to accept.* Daddy if

I must *I place my hand into his. All my pain subsides and my ability to breathe returns. My journey home begins.*

Not the End

You kept your promise, you came to escort me home.

My precious, precious baby girl I extend my hand not to guide you home, I'm just here to hold your hand through the pain and to remind you I am always with you. Do you want to be here?

The irony of it all, no! I don't need to tell you how happy I've been, I'm sure your witnessing. But if you save my baby and allow him or her to live, I will take this journey now.

Beth our heavenly father doesn't bargain - haggle to save one life over another. We all are of equal value in our maker's eyes. But my heart is full knowing you are willing to give your life for another.

Daddy the love I have for my baby can never be replaced and Kevin - my soul mate, he taught me what love is. No I don't want to be here.

I see, you've come a long way. *My father smiles.*

Beth you bring so much happiness to our son. For the first time in his life he wants more not only for himself but his family as well.

Amanda? Jackson? *Appearing in front of me, I begin to weep* your son….. If you don't know by now loves both of you.

Beth we know now. Tell our son we are the ones needing his forgiveness not the other way. It is Amanda and I who need to beg for his forgiveness. Our selfishness almost destroyed him. Let him know we are always with him.

I will….

Beth tell my baby boy his mother loves him. Let him know we have and will always be with him. Tell him his child - your child has his likeness in music, one song in particular. Tell him to remember the one I sang to him. Your baby will find comfort in it.

I will

My baby girl your about to embark on the next chapter of your life and with life, challenges will continue, death will happen and sorrow will show.

And I'm ready to confront and conquer. Daddy I finally have the will.

Yes you do but Beth danger still exist, adhere all signs.

Beth…..

Tears fall faster Rosa and my little Rosie every day I think of you two.

Beth we know you do. But we need you to let go of us, stop blaming yourself. Rosie and I can't move on – rest knowing you're not at peace with yourself.

Weeping It is so hard....

Beth difficult I'm sure but your baby needs all of you.

I will try but I will never forget either of you.

We know Beth, Rosie and I will always be with you. When you see your baby smiling just because, that will be Rosie and me sharing in your sweet joy.

Continue to take care of our son. We can finally rest in peace knowing he has let go of so much. When either of you are faced with challenges know we are looking after all three of you.

I will

Beth do you recall our heavenly father saying you had a purpose in life?

I do daddy

Well baby that purpose has not been fulfilled.

Smiling with tears continuing to fall Daddy does this mean my entrance into heaven is being denied once again? I'm being rejected.

Not rejected just not your time. But until that time my darling girl, live life to the fullest and do not let life challenges destroy who you have become, who you are destined to be. Now time for you to go back and meet your beautiful baby.

Diminishing from my sight We are all with you, always!